Emmy Grayson wrote her first book at the age of seven, about a spooky ghost. Her passion for romance novels began a few years later, with the discovery of a worn copy of Kathleen E. Woodiwiss's *A Rose in Winter* buried on her mother's bookshelf. She lives in the US Midwest countryside with her husband—who's also her ex-husband!—their baby boy, and enough animals to start their own zoo.

Also by Emmy Grayson

The Infamous Cabrera Brothers

His Billion-Dollar Takeover Temptation
Proof of Their One Hot Night
A Deal for the Tycoon's Diamonds

Discover more at millsandboon.co.uk.

A CINDERELLA FOR THE PRINCE'S REVENGE

EMMY GRAYSON

MILLS & BOON

First published in Great Britain 2022
by Mills & Boon, an imprint of HarperCollins*Publishers* Ltd,
1 London Bridge Street, London, SE1 9GF

www.harpercollins.co.uk

HarperCollins*Publishers*
1st Floor, Watermarque Building,
Ringsend Road, Dublin 4, Ireland

Large Print edition 2022

A Cinderella for the Prince's Revenge © 2022 Emmy Grayson

ISBN: 978-0-263-29555-9

09/22

MIX
Paper from
responsible sources
FSC **FSC™ C007454**
www.fsc.org

To Mr. Grayson, my mom,
and my dad, for once again
helping me get across the finish line.

To my editor, Charlotte.

To my fellow Harlequin authors,
who provide so much support
and camaraderie.

CHAPTER ONE

IT HAD TO be a sin to be that handsome.

Briony Smith watched Cass Morgan walk through the rowdy crowd of cowboys, ranch hands and the occasional tourist singing along with the Thursday night band. Normally on nights like this, she could barely hear herself think.

But as Cass flashed her a sexy smile, white against the dark tan of his skin, all she could hear was her own heartbeat thundering in her ears. His caramel-colored eyes locked on hers. She shivered. Every time his intense gaze landed on her, slowly sliding up and down her body, she was amazed that her clothes didn't melt off beneath the onslaught of his burning intensity.

The sensual feelings warred with her brain, had ever since Cass had walked into the Ledge a week ago, sat at the bar and kicked her newly discovered desires into overdrive. Her mother had drummed it into her for years that she didn't need a man to survive. But, she'd added with a cheeky wink as Briony had gotten older, that didn't mean you couldn't enjoy yourself.

"How'd negotiations go today?" she asked as Cass leaned on the bar. Jet-black hair curled over his collar. She threaded her fingers together so she didn't impulsively reach across the bar and run them through the thick, soft-looking waves.

Cass grimaced. Ever since he'd shown up last Thursday and ordered an old-fashioned, he'd been dropping hints at some business deal that had brought him to Kansas. One of the other bartenders, Katelyn, guessed it had something to do with a resort. Simon, the cook, was convinced Cass was opening his own cattle farm.

Briony glanced at him out of the corner of her eye, keeping her looking to a subtle glimpse instead of the flat-out ogling the other women of Nowhere had done all week. Although who could blame them? In a black polo fitted perfectly to his muscular torso and tan slacks, his cool confidence and blatant I-don't-give-a-damn attitude, he looked right at home among the dusty boots, torn jeans and plaid shirts favored by the locals who called this former logging town home.

"They went."

She arched a brow at the cryptic answer.

"So a double today?"

His grin returned and sent a jolt of electricity through her veins.

"Just a single."

She poured the expensive Scotch whiskey that had languished behind the bar for years, added an oversize ice cube and passed him the glass. She sucked in a breath as their fingers brushed. Judging by the devilish gleam in his eyes, he knew exactly what kind of effect he inflicted on her.

"How was your day?"

The magic of the moment disappeared. Her day had gone much as any day. She'd woken up early to make breakfast and drag her stepsisters out of bed. Once adorable little twins with blond curls, cherub cheeks and the sweetest disposi-tions, they'd morphed into sullen teenagers with a penchant for leaving dirty laundry around the house and responding to Bri's questions about school with grunts.

Small wonder, when they'd just lost the step-mother who'd loved them as her own to can-cer six months ago, the same disease that had claimed their birth mother when they were just three years old. Toss in a depressed father who spent his days parked in front of the TV with a beer clutched in his hand and the small house that had once been packed with love and laughter but now groaned under the weight of their family's despair.

Cheery.

"Briony?"

Cass's voice yanked her out of her melancholy state. She loved the way he said her name, the syllables rolling off his tongue in an exotic accent.

"Sorry." She gave him a quick smile. "It was fine."

Most people accepted that answer, didn't press for more out of courtesy or disinterest. But Cass stared at her, eyes probing. Her smile slipped as she shifted on her feet.

"What?"

"You're an open book."

She frowned. "Oh?"

He leaned across the bar. The scarred countertop still separated them. All she had to do was lean back to keep space between them.

But she didn't. No, she just stood there as he laid a finger on her rapidly beating pulse at the base of her throat. Amazing how much fire one graze of a fingertip could ignite, she thought desperately past the swirling rush of blood roaring in her ears. The first time he'd ever touched her, a mere tap of his finger, and she could barely stop from swooning like a teenager with her first crush.

"The pulse in your throat. Your tongue darting out to touch your lips." Despite the uptick in volume as the band transitioned into a raucous rendition of the latest country song, his words wound around her, a seductive spell. His eyes dropped down to her mouth. A wild temptation seized her, made her sway forward before common sense yanked her back. Had she truly almost kissed a customer? A most likely very wealthy, very handsome customer who would be leaving any day now?

Flustered, she grabbed one of the glasses she'd set out to dry as she stepped back from the bar and wiped it with the towel draped over her belt.

"Did something happen with your sisters? Or your stepfather?"

Her lips thinned. He'd overheard one of her phone conversations with Trey yesterday. He hadn't asked questions, but he'd heard enough of her side to glean that Trey had run up another astronomical bill that she was still trying to figure out how to pay without getting their electricity shut off.

"Maybe it was the polite version of 'I had a rough day but I don't want to talk about it.'"

When she looked back up, it was to see the intensity of Cass's gaze replaced with empathy. Her stomach dropped. Everyone in Nowhere knew her story, looked at her with drawn-down lips and crinkled eyes filled with pity. How could they look at her with anything else when just a week before Cass's arrival she'd had to drag her own stepfather out of the Ledge, drunk as a skunk and leaning on her as he'd sobbed her mother's name over and over again.

As much as she craved the help her neighbors sometimes offered, it wasn't worth the shame that would come when they saw how much of a hell her home had turned into. The sidelong glances she got now, the clucked tongues she overheard in the grocery store about how much suffering the Smith family had endured, all of it pressed on her, added to the pressure of being the sole provider for three broken people. She hated the darkness Trey had retreated into, the apathy her stepsisters had pulled around themselves like armor from the cruelties of the world.

Although, she acknowledged to herself, *they're not the only ones.* Despite her attempts to maintain a sunny facade in front of Trey and the girls, she had pulled back, too. She'd always existed on the fringes of the world created by her mother and Trey's marriage, putting on a face for her mother so Marie would never guess the depth of distance between her husband and daughter. Sometimes, if Briony had pretended hard enough, she had felt like they were all actually family.

Now she didn't even want to be a part of it all.

She winced. Just thinking that made her feel guilty.

She looked away from Cass. She didn't want pity from her neighbors, and especially not him. She'd wanted a flirtation and the chance to pretend that maybe, just for a little while, she could have a fairy tale instead of the nightmare her life had turned into.

"You can talk to me, Briony."

The words hung in the air, spoken in that seductive, honeyed voice. Her lips parted. What would it be like to confide in someone, especially someone like Cass who looked at her as if he saw her, truly saw her, and not just the persona she presented to the rest of the world?

Justin Lee and his sister Michelle wandered up to the bar, singing off-key.

"Bri!" Justin hollered. "Aren't you a sight for sore eyes."

"I'm surprised you can see straight," she retorted good-naturedly.

"Two more?"

"You got a ride?"

"Walking tonight." Justin clapped Michelle on the shoulder, who rolled her eyes. "My sweet baby sister is letting me crash on her couch."

Briony nodded to Cass.

"Be right back."

As she walked away, she felt Cass's gaze burning into her back. Their casual flirtation had deepened in the blink of an eye. She didn't know what to make of it, or him, for that matter. That she had almost slipped and confided in him should worry her. The fact that it didn't was even more concerning.

Perhaps she was just exhausted. Yes, exhausted and lonely. Otherwise she wouldn't be acting like this.

Because really, she thought with another quick glance at his dark profile, what did she actually know about him?

* * *

Cassius Morgan Adama prince of Tulay, watched his future wife pour beer into two frosted glasses. Fate had gifted him not only with a means to finally right the wrongs against his family and his homeland, but a stunning instrument with which to exact justice.

He'd seen photographs of her. None had done her fiery red locks, her bright emerald eyes or the cut of her stunning cheekbones justice. *Elfin* was a good word to describe her beauty, although *warrior* would also be appropriate, her arms slender yet muscular as she lugged trays and crates around the bar.

Yet what had stood out most to him was her smile. When he'd first walked into the dark interior of the Ledge last Thursday at three o'clock in the afternoon, Briony had turned around, flashed him a sunny grin and kindly yet firmly said, "Sorry, sir, we're closed until four. Be happy to serve you then."

When was the last time he hadn't been recognized? Fawned over? The brief flash of irritation had vanished, replaced by unexpected excitement and anticipation. He hadn't planned on revealing who he was to Briony, not yet, but he hadn't anticipated how satisfying it would be to be nobody for a while.

Briony's sassy sweetness had been an added bonus to her physical attractiveness. He'd known when he'd set upon this course that he risked being married to someone of unknown personality. Timid, vapid or even cruel; he'd dated plenty to be familiar with the negative qualities he might expect in a spouse.

But Briony was none of those things, at least not that he had seen in the last week. Judging by how easily she'd handled the crowds streaming through the bar, the occasional drunk or mouthy vacationer, Briony was anything but submissive. Yet she never made anyone feel small or set out to ridicule or embarrass them. She was just doing her job.

Satisfaction settled like a warm blanket over his shoulders. Yes, she would make an excellent wife and princess. The kind of woman his people could look up to and follow.

Unfortunately, he wasn't the only man to be drawn in by her. Judging by the sappy expression on the drunken Justin's face, he had also been attracted by her sparkling magic.

Among other attributes, he thought testily as Justin's eyes dropped down to Briony's chest.

His fingers tightened on his glass. If that clown had any idea who he was, who Briony was, he'd pick his jaw up off the floor, turn his eyes away from her stunning figure and slink off before Cass had him thrown in prison.

Steady. He was in America, not Tulay. And as much as the sight of that buffoon ogling Briony's backside, shown off to curvy perfection in slim-fitting blue jeans, irritated him, he had no desire to sink to the depths his future father-in-law, the King of Linnaea, had so frequently descended to. The man was a tyrant, like his father before him. The heir apparent, Alaric Van Ambrose, wasn't the despot his sire had been in his younger years. But the prince of Linnaea had a heart of ice that rivaled the freezing temperatures outside.

What would Briony think when she met her half brother and father for the first time? Two men who couldn't be more unlike her in every conceivable way, and from what the king had said, Briony had no idea they even existed. Her mother had concealed everything about her royal origins from her.

A slight smile curved his lips. He wished he could have met the woman who defied King Daxon Van Ambrose before she'd passed. Although judging by how firmly Briony handled the customers who got a little rowdy, the late Marie Smith, formerly Carmichael before she'd gone into hiding from her past lover, had taught her daughter well.

He pretended not to see Briony's green gaze flicker his way as she mopped up some beer Justin had splashed on the bar top. He'd accepted that once he'd discovered Briony's existence, he would be wed to the woman who would provide both revenge and salvation. It was his destiny.

The looming question, however, was whether or not Briony would accept hers.

CHAPTER TWO

BRIONY CLOSED THE door of the Ledge behind the last of the patrons and released a sigh that echoed in the cavernous room. The couple had hung on until the bitter end, well past the eleven o'clock closing time. She glanced down at her phone and sighed again.

Nearly midnight. And she had to get the twins up at six.

"You're nicer than I am."

Briony whirled around, wielding her phone above her head. Cass moved with lightning speed, one arm circling around her waist and drawing her flush against him as he grabbed her wrist and deflected the blow.

"Not the greeting I was expecting," he said, an amused smirk crossing his face.

"Why did you sneak up on me?" she demanded. She had intended to sound firm. Instead, she sounded breathless and husky. Her body had gone from fear to heightened awareness in the span of a heartbeat. Hard not to be aware when she could feel the hard muscles of his chest pressed against her breasts, his woodsy scent filling her senses as she inhaled sharply.

"I thought you saw me. I was sitting in the back corner."

She glanced in the direction he'd gestured. The corner booth was shrouded in shadow. Wariness flickered through her. Had he deliberately sat there so she wouldn't see him? So that he could stay undetected until the last guest left?

She shook off her sense of foreboding. It was late, and she was letting her imagination run wild.

"No, I didn't."

She'd been more disappointed than she should have been when she'd turned around after serving a group of hunters and found Cass's barstool empty. But she'd pushed through, focusing on filling drinks and not on glowing caramel-colored eyes that made her deliciously warm.

Slowly, Cass released his grip and stepped back, giving her space. She swayed forward before she caught herself. What was wrong with her? She never reacted like this to a man.

"I saw that you were the last one here." His voice carried a thread of steel, as if he was angry on her behalf. The thought touched her and filled her with a different, cozier kind of warmth. When had someone cared about her?

Not since Mom. The knowledge that he had stayed to make sure she was safe was like a balm to her bruised and battered heart.

"Gus, the owner, normally stays," she said past the lump in her throat. "But his wife just had a baby and she isn't sleeping well, so I told him to go home." She gestured to the snow-covered prairie outside the windows. "Not like we live in a dangerous city."

"You never know when danger might strike." With the way Cass was looking at her, she had a feeling that the biggest threat was standing less than three feet away. Not dangerous, she realized, at least not in that she feared he would harm her. But dangerous in that he was the kind of man who could make her throw her inhibitions to the wind and do something spontaneous.

"Anyway," he continued, "I thought you could use a hand."

She stared at him for a moment. "What?"

He gestured to the glasses lined up on the bar waiting to be cleaned and the bags of trash by the door.

"Help."

Her eyes slid from the crisp black polo molded perfectly to his broad shoulders down to his tan slacks and leather shoes. She'd bet his ensemble equaled a few nights' worth of tips at least. Not to mention he was a very mysterious, very wealthy businessman. Why on earth was he offering to help a lowly barmaid?

Before she could reply, he stepped forward and took her hand in his. Her lips parted on a gasp as he brought her fingers up and paused, his mouth a breath away from her skin.

"I get the impression that you excel at taking care of others." Could he feel the vibration that hummed through her body as he brushed a featherlight kiss across her knuckles? "But I'd like to help. Please, Briony."

The simple plea, combined with the way her name rolled off his tongue, crumbled her defenses as swiftly as if he'd wielded a battering ram. She should question the attention he was paying her.

Not just yet.

She wanted to enjoy the fantasy he offered, even if it was just for a night. Tomorrow would come soon enough, with its endless cycles of servitude and heartache. Tonight her world looked a little less bleak with Cass smiling at her with such warmth it made heat spread across her skin.

"Are you always so persuasive, Mr. Morgan?"

His eyes gleamed with promise. "When I see something I want, I'm relentless."

She blinked, her heart skipping a beat. Did he want *her*? Someone with his looks and obvious wealth could have anyone. But the way he was gazing at her, caramel-colored eyes smoldering, spoke volumes.

If he wanted just a short fling, what would she say? Her body very clearly screamed its answer, from her thundering pulse to the roaring in her ears. But her mind infiltrated the haze of want, reminding her that she didn't just feel physical attraction for this man. No, he had sparked something else, emotions that, even though she had never gone to bed with anyone, she was fairly certain she would struggle to keep out of any encounter with Cass.

"All right." She slowly withdrew her hand from his and focused on the safer topic. "Chairs on top of tables would be helpful. And trash goes in the dumpsters out back."

Judging by the quirk of his lips, her authoritative tone didn't mask the effect he had on her.

"Yes, ma'am."

Between the two of them, they made quick work of cleaning to the backdrop of jazz playing on the radio. Within thirty minutes, the bar was sparkling. She surveyed the freshly mopped floors and gleaming glasses with satisfaction.

"I can't believe how quickly we got that done."

"We make a good team."

She ducked her head to hide her blush. "Probably not what you were expecting to do on your trip."

Before he could respond, the soft strains of classical instruments filtered through the speakers. Briony smiled.

"I love this song."

Cass arched a brow. "Classical music?"

A moment later a woman's husky voice filled the bar, the lyrics spinning a seductive tale of spells and love.

Cass's eyes gleamed. He stepped toward her once more, his movements slow but intentional. She should run, before she did something stupid like let him touch her and drive the need that had seized her to a fever pitch she may not be able to pull away from him. Was the fantasy worth risking her heart when it was already so fragile?

But she didn't run. No, she let him slide an arm around her waist once more as her body leaned into him, molding to his muscular physique as if they'd been made for each other. He captured her hand in his, tan fingers threading through hers. The intimacy of his touch robbed the air from her lungs.

They started to sway, his other hand settling at the base of her back, his fingertips burning through the fabric of her shirt. When he leaned down and pressed his forehead to hers, the world shifted. His fingers slid up her spine, a gentle caress; it still made her arch deeper into his embrace. A thrill shot through her at his shaky intake of breath. Knowing she affected him emboldened her to slide her hand from his shoulder to the strong column of his neck. Heat radiated off his skin as his muscles tensed beneath her touch.

The singer's voice washed over them both, declaring her lover to be hers and hers alone. Cass's hands tightened on her as the words wrapped around them. The remaining thoughts at the edge of her conscience, to-dos and worries about the future, drifted away as she basked in the knowledge that after so long, someone wanted her again.

Her eyes drifted shut as her desire shifted, became clearer as her fear dropped away. She had never pictured her first lover as someone she'd known for such a short period of time, let alone someone she had no future with. She'd dreamed of that first joining being with a man she loved and who loved her just as deeply. While she certainly had strong feelings for Cass, she hadn't known him nearly long enough to be in love.

If Cass asked her to be with him tonight, what would she say? Was it worth turning him down to cling to her dream?

She opened her eyes as the last of the song faded, the only sound left their mingled breathing and the pounding of her heart. With his body pressed against hers, his heat seeping through her clothes, her dream barely held a candle to the sensual possibilities she glimpsed in his eyes.

Please kiss me.

Their gazes connected. Heat crackled between them. His eyes gleamed as a small smile tilted up the corner of his full lips.

"Can I buy you a drink?"

She laughed. "The bar's closed, sir."

He released her and walked back to her corner, circling around the counter as he grabbed one of her towels and tossed it over his shoulder. Normally she loathed anyone being in her space. But as she watched him survey the bottles on her shelf, she felt only a languid warmth. Being with him, letting down her guard and sharing herself with him, felt right.

Curiosity drew her closer.

"What are you making?"

"It's a surprise."

She tried to peek as he bent down to grab something out of the mini fridge. The sight of his perfectly sculpted rear distracted her. He straightened and resumed his secretive mixing. Judging by the smirk he shot over his shoulder, he knew exactly what part of his anatomy she'd been ogling.

"*Pour vous, mademoiselle,*" he said as he turned and set a glass in front of her. She picked it up and sniffed, the scent of brandy mixed with nutmeg relaxing her.

"I can't remember the last time I had a cocktail." She took a sip, closed her eyes and moaned as the creamy, chocolaty drink hit her tongue. "What is this?" she asked as she opened her eyes,

"A Brandy Alexander." Cass gestured to a dusty bottle behind him. "You had a passable cognac back here. Didn't want it to languish any longer."

"Thank you, Cass." She glanced down at the

shavings of nutmeg nestled on the frothy surface of her drink. One drink shouldn't matter so much.

But it did. Between working double shifts and cooking, cleaning and managing her stepfamily's existence, she couldn't remember the last time someone had done something just for her.

Warm fingertips grazed her cheek. Her head jerked up as Cass tucked a lock of hair behind her ear, a tender gesture she leaned into before she could stop herself.

"You strike me as the kind of woman who takes care of everyone. But," he whispered as he leaned in, his lips a breath away from hers, "who takes care of you, Briony?"

Me.

In a split second, she found herself caught between two worlds. Hopeless loneliness and a want so fierce it made her whole body ache.

A grim look settled on Cass's handsome face. "That's what I thought."

She jerked back, then tried to cover her movement with a casual sip of her drink.

"I'm very good at taking care of myself," she said with a flippancy she didn't feel.

"You are."

"And tonight you made me a drink." She shot

him an appreciative smile, trying to recapture some of their flirtatious chemistry. "After a long shift, I'd count that as being taken care of."

His gaze sharpened. She suddenly had the sensation she imagined one did when they realized they were in the sights of a predator.

Stop being melodramatic.

Yet she couldn't shake the sense that something was off. It wasn't just her horribly battered self-esteem talking, either. Why was a man of Cass's obvious wealth and sophistication in Nowhere, Kansas? Why had he taken an interest in her? And really, what did she know about him other than that he was from some country in the Mediterranean and liked high-end liqueur?

Cass leaned a little closer, so close she could see dark flecks in his eyes. It made them glitter in a way that was both erotic and unnerving.

"What if I could help you, Briony?"

"What?" she sputtered.

"Not just you," he continued as if they were having a normal conversation, "but your stepfather and stepsisters, too."

Slowly, she set her drink down so she didn't toss the contents in his face.

"In exchange for what?" she asked coolly. "Because it sounds like you're about to offer to make me your mistress or whatever they're calling it these days."

The intensity that had settled over Cass darkened as his eyes crackled with mahogany sparks of anger.

"I would never dishonor you that way." Her own anger dissipated as quickly as it had risen.

"Okay, then what are you suggesting?"

"What do you know about your father?"

The swift change in subject left her reeling.

"My father?"

"Yes."

A memory rose up, vivid and bitter. The one time she remembered her mother raising her voice. She'd been ten and had asked about her father for a school project.

There's nothing to tell, Mom said with an overly bright, brittle smile.

But—

Drop it, Briony. He never was, and never will be, a part of our lives.

At the time, she'd thought the emotion in her mother's voice had been anger. Mom's refusal to talk had hurt deeply and driven a wedge between them. While they had recovered, that conversation had lingered in the background of the remainder of their relationship. It had taken Mom's illness to make Briony conscious of the fact that she had been pushing her mother away, creating a distance as a shield against the hurt of not knowing that piece of her history. The realization had come in time for her and her mother to have a frank conversation, one that still hadn't resulted in her father's identity, but had left her feeling more connected to her mom than she had in years.

But as Briony reexamined the initial memory of her mother's refusal, she realized the truth: her mother had been afraid. She'd been so angry that she'd projected her own emotions onto her mother. It wasn't until now, revisiting the memory with the emotional maturity of an adult instead of the volatile feelings of a young girl, that she understood. It had been fear, not anger, that had made her mother's voice pitch up. Dread that made the tendons in her neck tense, the pulse in her throat pound so hard it was visible to the naked eye.

Warning whispered in her ear.

"What does my birth father have to do with this?"

Cass's smile flashed again, a cruel twist of his lips that made her feel cold. But she blinked, and it was gone. Had she imagined it?

"Your father has everything to do with what I'm about to propose." He reached over to a black briefcase sitting on the edge of the counter. He popped the lid and pulled out a folder. He slid it over to her. "Van Ambrose" had been written in bold black script across the top.

She swallowed hard. Intuition told her that whatever was in this folder had the power to change the course of her life. Mom had gone to great lengths to keep her father's identity a secret.

Yet her mother's unwillingness to talk about her birth father had left a void, a missing piece in Briony's life. Once her mom had married Trey and welcomed his daughters, Stacy and Ella, into the family, Briony had felt that emptiness even more acutely. Trey had been friendly, but the few moments of affection he'd displayed had felt like hard-won battles instead of fatherly love. She'd taken a shop class in high school because Trey had loved woodworking. The first time he'd spontaneously hugged her had been when she'd presented him with an end table she'd made for his birthday. When she'd overheard her mother and Trey arguing about his lack of involvement with Briony, she'd doubled her efforts to show her mom that everything was wonderful and see, she and Trey got along just fine.

The twins had been slightly better, coming into her room for slumber parties and going shopping with her up until she'd left for the university in Missoula. When she'd returned to help care for Mom, Stacy and Ella had been excited to see her.

But now…now there was nothing meaningful left in her life. Nothing but her father's true identity.

She tore open the envelope, not caring if Cass saw her shaking fingers or heard her shuddering breath. She pulled out a sheaf of photos. It took a moment for her to realize she was looking at pictures of her mom.

Tears pricked her eyes. Judging by her mother's long red hair and smooth face, the photographs had to be at least twenty years old. In every photo, she was in the company of a man who had to be in his mid- to late forties. Silver-haired with hawkish features, a smug smile and a lean figure dressed in expensive-looking suits, the expression on his face said he knew the world was his and dared anyone to tell him differently.

Yet in the few where he looked down at her

mother, his thin lips were softened at the corners, his arm wrapped possessively yet gently around Marie's waist.

Briony peered closer. His eyes were green. A vivid, almost unnatural emerald green. She knew without a doubt that she was finally seeing a photo of her father.

Blood roared in her ears as time slammed to a halt. She traced a finger over his face, happiness flooding her as she soaked in the matching eye color, the same pointed chin. Her mother and her had shared the same vivid red hair, but every time she'd seen a picture of the two of them together, the differences in their faces, it had been yet another reminder of the missing piece of her life.

Mom, why didn't you tell me?

Confusion swamped her happiness and sank it faster than she could catch her breath. Her eyes flickered to Cass as she felt herself drifting out to sea, unanchored and awash in grief and bewilderment. This man—a complete stranger—knew more about her past than she did.

She set the photos aside, reached back into the envelope and pulled out a sheaf of papers. Her mother's entire life was in her hands: her hospital records from when she gave birth to Briony in Kansas City, her college degree, her teaching contract for Nowhere's elementary school, the deed to their house, her and Trey's marriage certificate.

The last piece of paper made Briony's eyes grow hot. Her mother's death certificate. Had her father planned on finding Marie, making amends, only to find out too late that his lover had died?

Slowly, she looked up at Cass. "How did you get all this? Who are you?"

"Your half brother put together the file. He and your father gave it to me last month."

The photo edges crinkled as her fingers tightened. "You've met them? I have a half brother?"

"Yes, and yes."

"What's my brother's name?" she whispered.

"Alaric Van Ambrose."

"Alaric." She dropped the papers, grabbed the cocktail and tossed back half the contents. The warm slide of liqueur and cream took some of the edge off the whirlwind swirling inside her chest. She had a brother. A father. A family. Why had they never met? Had her father not wanted her? Had Mom known about her half brother?

"How long have they known about me?"

"Your father only found out about your existence last month. I expect your half brother only
knew for slightly longer than that, as he conducted his research."

Relief made her knees weak. If her father had
known about her all along and not sought her
out, she wouldn't have been able to bear the pain.

"Where are they?"

"In Linnaea."

She frowned. "I've never heard of it."

"It's a small country that lies on the coast of
the North Sea, wedged between Belgium and
the Netherlands."

Pride rang in his voice.

"You're from there."

Cass blinked in surprise before his handsome
features settled into a blank mask. "Originally,
yes. I've lived in the country of Tulay since I
was eight."

"I haven't heard of Tulay, either."

"Another small kingdom, a principality, between Spain and France along the shores of the
Mediterranean."

"Ah. Maybe you can draw a map of all these
countries I haven't heard of before sometime."
She winced. "Sorry. That sounded snarky. I'm
just…this is a lot to take in."

Cass reached over and grasped her hand, wrapped his fingers around hers. For a moment she resisted, her fingers stiff. But as she looked back down at the photos and papers scattered across the bar, she relaxed and accepted his offer of comfort.

She breathed out. "Okay. So my father gave you this?"

The hesitation was so slight she almost missed it. "Yes."

Her earlier wariness returned. Cass wasn't being entirely honest with her. "Why?"

"Because he needs your help."

"My help?" she repeated.

He handed her another envelope. This one was made of heavy cream material, an emblem of a key and sword crossed over a crown imprinted in the red wax seal on the back. Her fingers drifted over it. She'd seen this before once…an old envelope she'd found in the attic. The seal had been broken, the letters inside written in French. When she'd brought it to her mother, her mother had turned without hesitation and tossed it into the fire.

"Just old letters," she'd said casually. But Briony hadn't missed the tightness about her mother's mouth, nor the tense set of her shoulders.

"This seal…what is it?"

"The royal seal of Linnaea."

Her mind screeched to a halt. "Royal seal?"

"Your father is King Daxon Van Ambrose of the country of Linnaea. Your mother was his lover during the summer after her semester at Oxford."

Laughter bubbled up inside her. Once she started laughing, she couldn't stop, laughing so hard that tears threatened to roll down her cheeks. Cass watched her with an unblinking gaze, but she didn't care. He'd put so much into pulling an elaborate, albeit extremely cruel, prank on her.

"Who put you up to this?" she finally asked as her laughter subsided. "Did Gus do this? Or Jacques? Is this to get back at me for the shaving cream?"

"While I look forward to one day hearing about the shaving cream, I can assure you this is all very real."

She held up one of the photographs of her mother. "So my father is a ruler of a principality I've never heard of—"

"Country. He's a king, so Linnaea is designated as a country. Tulay is a principality overseen by a prince."

She waved his interruption aside. "Country, kingdom, whatever, which makes my mysterious brother a prince, too, and me...what? A princess? Heiress to a beautiful castle?"

Cass sighed. Her mirth and attempt at maintaining good humor despite the nastiness of whatever joke he was playing on her was swiftly replaced by anger.

"It sounds incredible, I know—"

"No," she said before she tossed back the rest of the cocktail and set the glass on the bar. "It sounds like the most awful joke someone has every played on me. I'm curious to know who gave you my mom's photo." She picked up another picture of her mom and the older man, arm in arm in front of the Eiffel Tower. "Seriously, this is some great Photoshop work."

Cass's eyes glittered dangerously. A shiver traced its way down her spine.

"This is no joke." His glacial voice rivaled the winter winds tearing across the prairie outside. "Thousands of people are depending on us."

"On us?" she repeated. "Who are you? Is your name even Cass?"

"It is. Short for Cassius Morgan Adama, a prince of the country of Tulay."

Her hand drifted back toward the glass. Maybe

he was actually unhinged and believed everything he was saying. It would certainly explain the conviction with which he spoke.

"The country of Linnaea is in dire financial straits. If you accept my proposal, you can help them, and I can help your family."

She stared at him for a long moment. He didn't give off a crazy vibe. But then how could any of this be true? Little girls dreamed of being secret princesses and one day being whisked off by their own Prince Charming.

But this was reality. Real life where fathers disappeared and mothers died and stepfamilies treated you like the scum on the bottom of their shoe.

"Fine. Humor me, and then I'm leaving. What exactly are you proposing?"

Cass reached down, then straightened and placed a blue velvet box on the counter. Briony stared at the box as her heart started to pound.

"Cass…"

He flipped the lid open to reveal a stunning diamond encircled by sapphires set in a silver band that screamed it was an antique. She didn't know how long she stared at the ring before she raised her shocked gaze to Cass's face. His eyes glinted once more with that predatory gleam, as if he'd cornered his prize.

"Marriage."

CHAPTER THREE

CASS RETURNED BRIONY'S stare with his own. Her emerald gaze dropped back to the ring, then up to him. The shock etched on her pale face would have been comical if there wasn't so much riding on this moment.

"Marriage," she finally repeated.

"Yes."

She whirled away from the bar, the scrunchie that had held her hair on top of her head giving way to the ferocity of her movements. Her fire-red curls tumbled over her shoulders and down her back.

God, she was glorious. Anticipation hummed in his veins as he circled the bar and followed her through a narrow doorway into a poorly lit room with lockers stacked against one wall.

What are you doing? He stopped, keeping distance between himself and Briony. He had indulged in the fantasy Briony had presented him when she'd flashed that grin, savored their flirtations and entertained vivid images of her spread naked across his bed.

But he was no longer Cass Morgan. No, he was back to being Prince Cassius Adama, and he had a job to do, a duty to fulfill. While sex would one day play a part in his and Briony's marriage, lust and any other chaotic emotions tied to love would only clutter up what he had to do. He would not make the same mistakes his father and Aunt Alecine had by succumbing to their feelings.

Briony stalked to one locker with a sunshine sticker peeling off the metal door, twirled the combination on the lock and wrenched it open. She yanked a threadbare green coat out and shoved her arms into the sleeves.

"Do you truly have no interest in who your birth father is?"

She spun to face him. Emerald fire snapped in her eyes. When he'd overheard Daxon and Alaric's argument and realized that Daxon not only had a secret daughter but was angry that one of his paramours had given birth to an illegitimate child, he'd known that marrying Daxon's daughter would cement his plan of revenge. Yet he'd also been confronted with what he'd known since he was ten years old: that his marriage would be a formal business arrangement. Aunt Alecine had told him plenty of times how her one attempt at love had resulted in his family's banishment.

A childhood memory clawed at him: Alecine hanging a red gingham blanket over the cracked window of the dingy one-bedroom apartment they'd barely managed to afford after fleeing Linnaea with nothing but the clothes on their back. It had been both a cheery splash of color against the drab walls and a stark reminder of what little they'd had. It had only lasted for a year, but it had been the hardest year of his life. Going hungry some nights had paled in comparison to knowing his mother had chosen her life of luxury over her husband and son, that their great love story had failed the test.

That year had been the catalyst for his nearly two decades of planning, of building up wealth as he watched Linnaea crumble into poverty. He'd resolved that on his thirtieth birthday he would go to Daxon and make him an offer, a financial agreement that would elevate Linnaea out of its looming economic depression while making Daxon beholden to the man he had banished as a child. Given that Daxon had not only forced Alecine, his former mistress, and her family to flee their home but had cut off their access to their finances and spread the word as far as Vienna that Alecine was a thief not to be trusted, putting a financial spin to his revenge had seemed appropriate. Still, Cass had always known that there was a risk that Daxon, whose pride was as legendary as his numerous affairs, would turn him down out of spite.

Enter Briony. He had been at a political summit in Paris, unaware that Daxon and Alaric had been invited until he'd arrived to represent his adopted country on behalf of Aunt Alecine's husband. He'd taken a call out in the hallway and seen Daxon and Alaric stalk by, their faces dark, voices low and heavy with anger. He'd followed and, once they'd disappeared into a small conference room, stationed himself outside the door.

"...the right thing to do. By all accounts, she's in dire financial straits."

"I didn't even know she existed until you did your little pet project."

Daxon's voice had roughened with his illness, the angelic quality that had supposedly seduced scores of women now a harsh rasp as he snapped at his son.

"That's not my problem," Alaric had replied in a tone that could have frozen hell. "But if you—"

"Tell you what, *son*. If she can save the country from financial ruin or find me a cure, I'll reach out. Otherwise, I want nothing to do with a bastard child."

Just like, that puzzle pieces had fallen into place. A week later, Cass had instructed his plane to land at the private airport near the Linnaean palace. He'd been greeted by a contingency of Daxon's palace guards and taken straight to the king himself. Every time he remembered the selfish buzzard's face dissolving from smug satisfaction at having arrested a member of the Adamos family to fury mixed with grudging acceptance that what Cass was offering was a deal he couldn't afford to pass up, he savored the thrill of having finally bested the man who had ruined not only his life, but his father's and aunt's lives as well.

Cass had known there was a good chance Daxon would say no, convince himself he could somehow still drag the country out of the hole he'd dug for it with his relentless spending.

But it was that same pride that made Daxon say yes when Cass presented his offer. If Daxon didn't accept Cass's financing and offer of marriage, not only would Linnaea continue to march toward an economic depression, but word would eventually leak of Briony's existence. How, Cass had asked, would Daxon handle the press fall-out, that he'd known about his daughter struggling to make ends meet in some godforsaken little town while he dined in the lap of luxury?

"You're blackmailing me?" Daxon had demanded before he collapsed into coughing.

"I don't have to," Cass had replied silkily. "Your son is already furious that you would deny her. How long do you think it will take before he reaches out to her if you don't? What if he leaks it to the press? Or she does, once she learns the truth? Compare that to not only embracing your long-lost child but forming an alliance that will save the people of your country?"

He'd arched a brow as Daxon's reply was lost in another hacking cough. Slowly he'd advanced on the old man. For a brief moment, as a child, he'd feared the legendary Daxon Van Ambrose, the man with so much power he'd driven Cass's father from his own home and sent his mother fleeing to her wealthy relatives in Paris.

But every step he'd taken toward the throne, toward the hunched figure of a dying coward, had emboldened him until he'd been less than a foot away.

"How long do you have left, my king? A year, maybe less?"

The glare Daxon had thrown at him had confirmed that the disease was spreading faster than any doctor could contain.

"How will you be remembered? As a savior? Or as the devil?"

Briony would help Cass not only achieve his revenge but bring Linnaean back from the brink of ruin. In turn, he would rescue her and her family from looming poverty.

Besides, what woman wouldn't jump at the chance to become a princess?

He'd never once been tempted by notions of love or romance. Family, duty and honor mattered above all.

"Who the hell do you think you are?" she demanded. He stood his ground as she advanced on him and jabbed a finger at his chest. "You waltz into my bar, flash your money and make me feel…"

"Make you feel what, Briony?"

"Special," she finally snapped. "Like you were interested in me and found me attractive."

"I am interested, and I do find you attractive."

She snorted. "Sure. And I'm a long-lost princess, my birth father is a king, and you're a prince who can rescue my home country by marrying me."

"You truly think I would make up an elaborate joke like this, propose marriage to you, just to hurt you?"

It may not be a joke, but you're still lying to her. Using her.

He pushed the unexpected thought away. There was too much at stake for him to suffer an attack of conscience now. Besides, it wasn't just his own personal vendetta on the line. The fate of thousands of Linnaeans rested on his shoulders.

"People I've cared about have done worse things."

The pain in her voice tugged at him. He took a cautious step forward. His arm came up, his fingers reaching out to caress her shoulder, do something to offer a modicum of comfort.

Stop.

His arm dropped back to his side.

"I'm not. This is real. You can trust me, Briony."

Doubt flickered through him as she hesitated. He had never not succeeded. Victory came to him as naturally as breathing.

"Look me up, Briony. I assure you, I speak the truth about my background and yours. My offers of marriage and helping your family are genuine."

Slowly, she pulled her phone out.

"Prince Cassius Morgan…"

"Adama. Of Tulay."

Her fingers flew over her phone. Then she froze. Her eyes flickered back and forth over the screen. Had she found the numerous articles detailing his life? The gossip columns hazarding guesses as to who he was dating? Or had she found the website that was his aunt's pride and joy, the official site of the royal family of Tulay?

At last, she looked at him, her eyes opaque.

"So am I supposed to curtsy or what?"

The curt yet sassy response startled a laugh from him.

"A curtsy is not necessary."

A harsh breath escaped her as she ran her fingers through her hair, further tousling the curls. He had a sudden vibrant image of her laid naked across his bed at the palace in Tulay, the setting sun painting his suite with rose-gold light as he buried his fingers in her hair and kissed that pert mouth.

"So…this is real."

"It's real."

She typed something else into her phone. A

moment later she blew out another breath that bordered on a growl.

"What?"

"Just looked up 'Daxon,' 'Alaric' and 'Linnaea.' It…it all checks out." She glanced up at him and frowned. "You don't need to look so smug."

"Don't I?"

She sank down onto a bench and shoved her phone into her coat pocket.

"You can't blame me for being suspicious."

"I don't."

"Just because you have photos of my mother with…*him* doesn't mean I'm actually his daughter. And you could have forged the letter."

"And if you agree to accompany me tomorrow, we will have a DNA test performed immediately. But," he added, "when you see his eyes, will you be able to deny what your heart already knows?"

She swallowed hard.

"There is a…slight resemblance."

More like a carbon copy. Daxon and Alaric both possessed the emerald-colored eyes of the Van Ambrose royals. Once Briony was standing next to her father and brother, there would be no question about her parentage.

"You said if I accompany you tomorrow. What are you talking about?"

He eased himself down onto the bench across from her. This was a step in the right direction, but he had to tread carefully. One wrong move and he could lose his chance.

"The letter from your father asks if you will become my wife to ensure a financial alliance that will rescue Linnaea from an economic depression. If you agree, you'll accompany me to Linnaea to meet your father and brother, as well as formally announce our engagement."

Her laugh this time came out strangled.

"Our engagement? You barely know me."

"I know enough."

"Right. That I'm the daughter of a king."

The bitterness in her voice crept under her skin.

"That's part of it," he said honestly. "But as I said, this would be a mutually beneficial arrangement, and not just for Linnaea. I have paperwork ready to establish trust funds for both of your stepsisters that would ensure their financial security and a private counselor who would be available to them as long as they need to process their grief over your mother's death. Your medical and credit card debts would be wiped away. I also have a reservation on standby for Trey at an exclusive rehabilitation clinic in Kansas City with an extraordinary success rate."

She leaned forward, her hair falling in a red curtain over her face.

"You told me yesterday when I overheard your conversation that you just wanted them to get better. This is your chance to make that happen."

He knew the reminders of her home situation were calculated and heartless. But she needed to be reminded of her situation and of what he had the power to do.

"And in return I marry a stranger."

He reached out and grabbed her hand. Her head snapped up as tension crackled in the air between them. She stared down at his fingers threaded through hers, then slowly looked up at him.

He was a heartless bastard. But God help him, he couldn't stop.

"In return, I can offer you several things. Meeting the remaining family you have. A life of luxury and ease. Children. A chance to have your own family. I won't pretend that I'm capable of offering love, but I can offer a pleasant relationship between two people who are obviously attracted to each other, which bodes well for certain aspects of the marriage."

Her cheeks turned pink.

"We don't know each other well." He was treading on dangerous ground. But, he argued with himself, he was making his case, not indulging in his own attraction. "But I already know much about you."

"From your research," she whispered. He smiled. She was trying to keep him at bay. But he had started this battle, and he intended to finish it.

"Yes. Research that also showed me that you're loyal to your family, although by all accounts you have every right to walk out and leave them to their own misery."

She shook her head. "I can't do that. They're grieving."

"You're compassionate."

He meant that. It was a quality he'd normally eschewed as weak. Yet on Briony it didn't seem like weakness. No, on her it came across as strength.

"And," he added with a smile, "you handle drunks with the grace of a queen."

She laughed. Desire urged him to lean forward

and claim her mouth, give her a demonstration of just how compatible they could truly be.

But not yet. Patience. It had taken more than he had expected to convince her that he was in fact a prince, that her father was a king and that she was a princess. If he frightened her off now, he might lose his chance.

And, he reminded himself as he released her hand and straightened, he'd lusted after women before. As enjoyable as those encounters had been, the actual event often paled in comparison to the anticipation that preceded it. Sex had become more of a routine, the occasional sojourn into physical pleasure a way to take the edge off after a long day of running his business enterprise or supporting Aunt Alecine or his father in their political endeavors.

Bedding Briony, while pleasurable, would most likely follow the same pattern. If he could hold on to that thought, his attraction would dim, and he could once again focus on the task at hand.

"Will you come with me to Linnaea?"

Briony sighed. "When would we leave?"

"Tomorrow at ten a.m."

She blinked. "Tomorrow's Saturday. I work."

"If you agree to my proposal, you'll never have to work again."

A scowl crossed her face. "And you think that sounds appealing? To lounge around and do nothing all day?"

He shrugged. "Given your and your family's circumstances, yes."

She surged to her feet. "How dare you!"

He stood, trying to keep a lid on his own temper. He was offering her not only a solution to her every problem, but the chance to finally meet her birth father. Based on what little she'd shared over the last week, she craved knowledge of her lineage, a chance to have blood relatives once more. She didn't know the weasel was a blight on the face of the earth. So what could possibly be leading to this unexpected and frustrating last-minute display of temper and resistance?

"How dare I what, Briony? Offer you everything you and your family need? Offer you the one thing you want?"

"At the cost of marrying someone I met less than a week ago!" she cried. "Coming in and offering to rearrange my life. I've done just fine on my own."

"Have you?" he asked softly as he stood and towered over her. "Your house is one delinquent payment away from foreclosure. Just yesterday your stepfather ran up over a thousand dollars in online gaming debt." Briony blanched, but he didn't let up. Not now, not when she needed to see how much she needed him and what he could do for her. "Between caring for him and your stepsisters, when will you be able to finish your education degree? Five years, ten? Perhaps never?"

"How I manage my life and my family's life is none of your concern," Briony bit out before she turned and fled the locker room.

He breathed in deeply, steadying himself. The hunter in him demanded that he chase her, stop her, not let her leave until he had her signature on the contract. But the planner in him knew better. To do so would only push her away. Her fierce reaction betrayed her innermost thoughts; she knew he'd spoken the truth. All he had to do was be patient. She would come around.

And if she doesn't?

His measured steps led him out into the bar just as Briony was heading for the front door. The sight of the files in her hand and his briefcase standing empty on the counter lessened some of his unease. If she was taking the papers, she was still intrigued, even if she didn't want to be.

"My plane leaves at ten a.m. tomorrow morning from the airstrip just outside of town," he said as she jerked the door open. "If you're not there by a quarter to ten, I'll assume you have rejected my offer."

"You can let yourself out the kitchen door," she retorted. "I set the alarm. If you're not out in five minutes, you'll get a personal visit from the Nowhere Police Department."

"Not very friendly to outsiders, I'm guessing?"

She stood framed in the doorway, snow swirling behind her as a winter wind teased her red curls.

"Good night, Prince Cassius. Have a safe flight."

With a final glare, she slammed the door behind her. He stared at it for a long minute before grabbing his briefcase off the counter and heading for the kitchen door. While it would be a simple matter to smooth over his presence at the bar with the local police, he'd had enough disagreements for the evening.

He glanced back at the front door of the bar, an unexpected smile lurking about his lips. Based on Alaric's file, he had anticipated a quick and breathlessly grateful "yes" to his proposal, perhaps even a few appreciative tears. Not the display of furious independence or the grand exit into the cold.

She would be there tomorrow morning, he thought as he turned the lock and let himself out the kitchen door. Without him, her family would plunge into ruin within months, if not weeks.

His mind conjured up the last image of her framed in the doorway, red curls splayed across her shoulders, emerald eyes flashing fire, lush lips set into a firm line as the snow swirled behind her. Even in her worn coat and jeans, she'd exuded a regal fortitude befitting the descendants of royalty and a frustrating yet admirable stubbornness.

She might not show. A possibility he had not accounted for. But the thought didn't fill him with anger or concern. His smile grew as he walked around the bar toward the snow-covered parking lot.

The possibility of going deeper into battle to make Briony Van Ambrose his wife filled him with a heated excitement. No matter what happened tomorrow morning, she would be his.

CHAPTER FOUR

BRIONY APPROACHED Nowhere Regional Airport at 9:46 a.m., a scowl on her face and a duffel bag slung over her shoulder. Resigned anger churned in her gut as she walked toward the tiny building and the plane looming behind it. When she'd walked out of the bar last night, it had been with every intention of never seeing Cass again.

But as her rush of adrenaline had abated on her walk home, doubt had crept in as the winter wind pierced her cloak and chilled her skin. What could she do on her own? Trey was still gambling. She wouldn't be able to work enough shifts to cover both his debts and the bills. A move to a larger city and a better-paying job was out of the question. The twins would fight her tooth and nail, and Trey probably wouldn't be much better.

She could just leave on her own. She'd dreamed of it more than once. But every time she seriously contemplated it, she knew she could never just leave her stepfather and stepsisters to drown in their own misery. The guilt alone would plague her the rest of her life.

And it wouldn't be what her mother would have wanted.

Although, she'd conceded with sorrow as she'd trudged through snowdrifts piling up on the sidewalks, did she really know what her mother would have wanted? Marie Smith had had an entirely different life before she'd fled Europe, one she'd concealed from Briony and most likely from Trey, too. And if Cass's story was to be believed, she'd hidden Briony's birth from her father.

Out of everything that had been revealed last night, that had cut the deepest of all. Her mother had always been a proponent of honesty and tough conversations. Even when they had been uncomfortable, she'd preferred to be up-front and truthful.

So why, when she'd known how much Briony had longed to know more about her history, when she'd seen Briony and Trey struggle to form a relationship, had she concealed so much? What had frightened her so much? Had she been scared of her former lover? Or worried that if Briony knew the truth she'd be hurt, even angry?

She remembered the moment she'd confided to her mother when she'd come home how much the conversation about her father all those years ago had hurt, how Mom had cried and said she was sorry that she'd hurt her and that if Briony could just trust her, it had been done out of love. Briony had accepted it, grateful that they were putting the pain behind them and savoring the few months they had left.

That bittersweet memory was now tainted.

Those thoughts had been swirling around in her head as she'd let herself into the house at two in the morning. Dishes had been piled in the sink. Dirty clothes had been tossed in a heap outside the laundry room. The twins had tracked in snow that had melted into slushy gray puddles on the scarred hardwood floors.

And Trey... Trey had been snoring in the armchair, multiple empty beer cans littering the floor around him. The family computer in the den had been open to an online poker site. She'd tried to haul Trey out of his chair. At first, he'd just snored, the stench of stale beer making her sick to her stomach. Finally, after she'd pulled him to his feet, he'd opened bloodshot eyes.

"Marie?" he'd whispered.

Briony's heart had clenched. She'd started to

respond when suddenly his eyes had narrowed in anger.

"It's just you. God, I wish you had died instead."

Perhaps she'd just grown numb enough that his words hadn't initially hit. She'd managed to drag him down the hall to his bedroom and lay him on the bed, where he'd promptly passed out again. She'd made it out into the hallway where she'd slid down against the wall, tears slipping down her face.

The final straw. Just in time for a dark-haired, amber-eyed seducer to come along and offer her a deal. A deal that, as she'd sucked in a shuddering breath and wiped away her tears, finally started to sink in.

She'd read and reread the contract, then read it once more before she'd walked out the door. The wedding would take place in the next eight weeks.

Eight weeks, she thought, trepidation mixed with a dash of nervous excitement. She'd always dreamed of getting married, of having a family. Even after the lackluster ending to her one college relationship, she'd still imagined her marriage having roots in love and companionship.

But without Cass's offer, she wouldn't be getting married anytime soon, much less living her life outside the tiny little circle she existed in now. Cass had a plan and the money to help not just her, but Trey and the twins, make a fresh start. He was also offering her the chance her mother never had, to meet not just her birth father but a brother who had been interested enough in her existence to search for her. Even though it stung that neither had come to Kansas, it probably wouldn't have been easy for the king or the prince of a country to suddenly travel to America. Not if things were as dire as Cass had depicted them. What little news she'd found had painted a similarly grim picture. While Alaric and Daxon mostly kept to themselves and were rarely photographed outside of Linnaea, the most recent articles had speculated on the rising inflation, labor strikes and a recent layoff of teachers.

Linnaea was in trouble. But as she'd flipped through the articles, then the photos as the sky had lightened and night had given way to early morning, she'd found herself feeling…hopeful. There had even been a touch of excitement as she'd packed her bag. A new adventure loomed on the horizon, a chance to find herself and learn more about who she was.

Not to mention marriage to a man who had

frustrated her to no end last night but still sparked the most intense attraction she'd ever experienced.

She swallowed past the sudden lump in her throat. She'd been ready to give herself to Cass last night, to suggest they head back to his hotel or wherever he was staying. Last night it had been sexy, a sensual fantasy. Now, even though the thought of him still sent a frisson of awareness down her spine, the contractual nature of what would become their future relationship tempered the romance.

She hadn't just dreamed of marrying for love. No, she had dreamed of her first time being with a man who adored her. Cass had made it clear that he wouldn't be feeling much of anything for her.

There was a measure of sorrow that she would never have the fairy-tale love. But, she reminded herself, she was gaining so much. The chance to know the other half of her family. The chance to be free from the crushing weight of debt. The chance to start her life anew. And anytime she started to feel too much sadness or regret, she just replayed Cass's words over and over again in her mind:

I won't pretend I'm capable of offering love...

Each replay helped her bury any emotions she had felt for Cass Morgan deep down and focus her attentions on other things.

A gust of wind barreled across the prairie and hit her in the face as she walked around the airport. She burrowed her chin deeper into her scarf. Time to focus on the positives. At least she would be marrying a man she got along with and was physically attracted to. She might not have the love story, but her wedding would do something few marriages could ever do: make a difference.

Everything Cass had told her last night had checked out, at least with what she'd been able to find online. Numerous articles touted Cass and his family, royalty of the Mediterranean state of Tulay. Their origins were murky, barely touched on in what she'd read aside from a vague reference about them having lived in Linnaea in the past. But since Cass's aunt Alecine had married the prince of Tulay, the family seemed to have gained the Midas touch. Everything from oil and manufacturing to shipping and banking. Their estimated wealth was in the billions.

That spark of suspicion she'd felt last night crackled across the back of her neck again. If Cass was so wealthy, why did he need to marry her? Why not just give the money to Daxon? One of many questions she had for Cass on their flight to wherever it was he was taking her.

She'd pored over Daxon's letter so many times she nearly had it memorized. Written in a strong, bold script, Daxon had written out the exact same situation Cass had described: a country on the brink of ruin, a financial alliance by marriage and a chance for her to get to know the other half of her family. He had also explained that her mother had become overwhelmed by life in the spotlight and hadn't told him about her existence. It hadn't been until Alaric, her half brother, had come across a letter from an old palace physician noting Marie's positive pregnancy test that they had even suspected Marie had had a child after she'd left Linnaea and returned to the States.

Daxon's letter had been polite but friendly, the kind of cautious wording she would expect from a man who had never met his long-lost daughter. Perhaps it was Daxon's own tempered voice that had tamped down some of her own excitement at finally meeting her father. Or perhaps she'd just had enough of getting her hopes up only to have them dashed.

Or, she acknowledged with a frown, perhaps it

was the unease that invaded every time she remembered her mother's fear. Daxon's claim that life in the spotlight had scared her mother off seemed plausible. But she had a hard time envisioning that as the cause behind Marie's flight from Europe. Had the stresses of royal life truly spooked her mother so badly that she'd not only moved back to America but changed her last name?

So many unanswered questions, Briony thought with a sigh.

Her boots crunched in the snow as she neared the tarmac. The runway had been cleared of any snow—a feat, given that it had still been snowing at 6:00 a.m. when she'd roused the twins from bed for school. When she'd told them she was leaving to take care of some family business and that Trey's sister Debra would be coming to stay with them awhile, they had barely even looked at her.

"Fine," Stacy had grumbled.

"Whatever," Ella had echoed.

They hadn't even asked how long she'd been gone.

She approached a man dressed in black pants and a burgundy winter coat standing guard over the plane's stairs. He bowed so low she nearly jumped back so his military-style hat didn't smack her in the face.

"Good morning, Your Highness."

"Um…you can just call me Briony."

The man didn't bat an eye. "Welcome, Princess Briony."

"Just Briony," she repeated with a smile to soften the edge in her voice. "Being called a princess is a little weird at the moment."

"It's who you are. Might as well get used to it, Your Highness."

She stiffened as the familiar husky voice drifted down to her. Slowly she looked up to see Cass framed in the door of the plane, a smile of satisfaction on his handsome face. Her fingers tightened around the strap of her duffel bag. She was grateful for everything he was offering. But the smugness in his expression rankled. What would he do if she turned and walked away? Chase her down? Throw her in the dungeon?

Or perhaps worse, let her walk all the way home back to her living nightmare of loneliness and rejection?

She lifted her chin. She was making the right decision.

"Good morning to you, too, *Prince* Cass." She dipped into a deep, overexaggerated curtsy. The guard made a noise that almost sounded like a suppressed laugh. But when she glanced at him, his face was as smooth as alabaster.

Cass came down the steps. Dressed in black pants and a long matching peacoat, the collar pulled up against the cold, he exuded a dark mystique that froze her in place.

He stopped just inches away from her, amber eyes fixed on her face. The same woodsy scent that had made her sway on her feet last night as he'd cradled her in his arms during their dance wound about her and filled her with warmth that not even a winter's chill could steal.

"Let me help you with that."

His voice wrapped around her, slipped into her blood and left her dazed as he took the duffel bag off her shoulder and gestured for her to go up the stairs.

Stay detached. Don't fall for him just because he's hotter than sin.

"After you, Briony."

She stared at the first step. As soon as she walked up, there would be no going back. She would be sealing her fate, traveling outside of the country for the first time, meeting her father and the brother she never knew she had, and agreeing to marry a man she'd known for barely a week. Not just any man, but a prince, an actual real-life prince, with secrets.

She glanced back once more at Nowhere a mile or so in the distance, the buildings like tiny dollhouses dusted with snow surrounded by the endless prairie. She should feel something, a sense of loss, sadness, homesickness.

But this place hadn't been home for a very long time.

She turned away and walked into the plane.

Cass watched with satisfaction as Briony gaped at the luxury laid out in front of her. Oval windows marched down either side of the plane and let in bright afternoon sunlight that lit up the creamy interior. Four white leather seats were clustered around a tabletop. Across the aisle, a flat-screen TV displayed a news channel. The second half of the main area boasted two more seats and a long sofa, complete with bright red and blue pillows to make the interior more welcoming. A partition concealed the rest.

"People actually live like this?"

Cass chuckled. She moved farther into the plane, stepping gingerly on the plush carpeting.

"They do. Soon you will, too."

"Sir, we're preparing for takeoff," a voice crackled over a speaker in the ceiling.

Cass pressed a button on his armrest. "Five minutes, Martin."

"Yes, sir."

Cass reached into his briefcase and pulled out a copy of the contract Briony had taken with her last night. He set it on the table and laid a pen on top.

"What is that?"

"The contract stating that you will enter into an engagement with me and that we'll be married within eight weeks."

He watched as she sucked in a deep breath and ran a hand through her hair.

"What if something changes?"

"Like if you change your mind?"

"Yes."

He shrugged. "There is a clause in there stipulating the agreement can be nullified if both parties agree and sign an addendum. Then I return you to Nowhere and your life goes back to the way it was."

Those green eyes narrowed, hardened. "But Trey gets kicked out of the facility and the girls lose their trust funds?"

"Why you would want anything good for them

after the way they've treated you is beyond me," he retorted with an edge to his voice. Did she truly think him so callous that he would pull a grieving alcoholic out of his treatment program? "But no. Regardless of how things progress between us, Trey's stay will be paid for and your stepsisters will have trust funds established."

She blinked in surprise. "Really?"

He gritted his teeth as he stretched his lips into a small, benevolent smile. "Really."

Some of the worry eased from her face. But he still detected a couple tense lines about her eyes as she glanced down at the contract again.

"Briony..."

Slowly, she looked up at him. The uncertainty in her gaze tugged at him once more.

"This is your choice."

Her eyes gleamed for a moment before she blinked rapidly and looked down.

"I know it is."

Pain roughened her voice. He hadn't missed the look she'd cast her hometown before she'd climbed on the plane. What thoughts had gone through her mind? What dreams had she had before they'd been snatched away by death and loss?

Before he could respond, she grabbed the pen.

The nib dashed across the paper with a ferocious swirl. She tossed the pen down and brushed past him.

He stared down at her signature. He'd expected to feel pride, excitement, something. One more hurdle had been cleared in the goal he'd been working toward for as long as he could remember.

Yet all he felt as he turned to see Briony sit toward the back of the plane and stare out the window was a hollow sensation in his chest.

When the clock had hit nine forty-five this morning, he'd felt an unexpected wave of disappointment. He'd anticipated a last show of resistance. But a flat-out refusal? The tightness around his lungs had eased a minute later when he'd seen the tangle of red curls and that faded green coat against the stark white of a winter prairie landscape moving toward the plane. It had confirmed one of his talents, that of reading people and sometimes knowing them better than they knew themselves.

However, he conceded, as he took a seat farther down the plane to give her space, in this case he'd only been partially right. Judging by the tense set of her shoulders and the fierce line of her jaw, Briony wasn't completely confident in her decision. Just signing the contract wasn't enough to ensure she'd follow through. Technically he could hold her to the terms all the way until they said "I do."

But he wasn't a monster. If she truly changed her mind, he wouldn't carry her kicking and screaming down the aisle.

His eyes drifted down her body, lingering on the swells of her breasts beneath her sweater and her long legs encased in blue jeans. He steepled his fingers as a slight smile tugged at his lips. Between the luxury he had to offer her, taking care of her family and the chance to be reunited with her father and brother, he had plenty of weapons at his disposal. He knew, too, judging by the way she'd reacted to him on the steps, that her attraction to him hadn't been completely destroyed by last night's revelations. No, it simmered just below the surface. Something he could use if necessary.

The door to the plane was shut as the engines hummed. His smile grew as the plane taxied down the runway and took off, soaring above the snow-dusted fields. He had Briony exactly where he needed her. In eight weeks, she would be his wife.

And he would finally have his revenge on the Van Ambrose royals.

CHAPTER FIVE

AN HOUR LATER, Briony had barely moved. Cass had conducted some business on his laptop, expecting her to pepper him with questions about her family, royal life, anything but the silence that permeated the cabin.

It bothered him, he realized with some annoyance. Yes, he was getting something out of their arrangement, but didn't she realize that he was rescuing her and her ungrateful stepfamily? That between his wealth and social standing he could literally offer the fairy tale that so many were raised on yet never got to experience?

One of his flight attendants, Sarah, entered with glasses of sparkling water. Briony stirred long enough to accept a glass and thank Sarah with a gracious smile. But as soon as the flight attendant disappeared, she went back to being stone-faced.

He sighed. "Are you going to sulk the whole flight?"

She glanced at him from beneath her lashes. "I just left the only home I've ever really known and am flying into an unknown future. I think I'm allowed some time to 'sulk,' as you put it, although I thought of it more as taking time to process the monumental changes in my life."

Of course she would need time. Irritated at himself for taking her silence so personally and jumping to erroneous conclusions, he opened his mouth to apologize.

"Not to mention I signed a contract to marry someone I've known less than a week. Actually," she said as she leaned forward, "make that less than twelve hours. I thought I was getting to know Cass Morgan. You still haven't apologized for lying to me."

His regret disappeared.

"I didn't lie."

It was ridiculous that her statement should cause a tensing of his muscles, especially since he was keeping secrets from her. He hadn't outright lied, but he had certainly played a game with the words he'd spoken last night. She didn't know that he had been the one to offer the solution to Daxon, instead of the other way around. She didn't know about his personal vendetta against the Van Ambrose royals. And she had no idea that not only was her father a self-absorbed monster, but he didn't care about her existence unless it benefited him.

Something in his chest twisted as he watched the woman across from him. He hadn't told her of Daxon's illness, and judging by her lack of questions, Daxon hadn't addressed it in the letter he'd included with the file. Even if Daxon was a monster, what would it do to Briony learning that her father was most likely going to die within a couple years of her mother? Was he doing the right thing, exposing her both to the pain of yet another loss and Daxon's horrid, selfish nature?

You'll be with her. Even though theirs would be a marriage of convenience, and it would obviously take some time to regain the camaraderie they had enjoyed when he had simply been Cass Morgan, he would protect her from Daxon, be there to support her with whatever the future dealt.

He would never be able to love her. Love, as he'd observed, could make a person deliriously happy...until it didn't. It could twist into something dark and angry, like it had with Aunt Alecine and Daxon, so-called love turning to hatred. Or it could be enough until it wasn't, like it had with his mother. It had been much easier for his mother to go against her parents' wishes as a young woman with stars in her eyes and marry an aspiring lawyer from a decent family than to flee with a king's accusations of betrayal hanging above her head.

Even if love didn't destroy, it didn't last. When he told Briony he would never be able to love her, he meant it. But that didn't mean he would leave her at the mercy of Daxon. In less than sixty days, she would be his wife. She would be family. And he protected family.

"Understandable after the numerous bombshells I've dropped on you."

Surprise flashed in her eyes, followed by a tiny smile of thanks.

"It's a lot to take in. And I don't like that you misrepresented yourself."

He tamped down his guilt and spread his hands in a gesture of openness. "Ask away. What do you want to know?"

"Why do you want to marry into the royal family so badly?"

He covered his surprise at her bold question with a sip of water. He turned her words over in his mind, trying to decide how best to address a natural yet loaded query.

No matter what, he couldn't tell her the whole truth yet. Would she have any interest in meeting her father once she learned how cruel he could be? Or would she decide that life with her selfish stepfamily would be at least marginally better?

Cass had been eleven years old when he, his father and his aunt had fled Linnaea under cover of darkness before King Daxon had tossed them in prison. Cass's father, Leopold Adama, had committed only one crime: he'd been the brother of Alecine Adama, Daxon's latest mistress. Alecine may have fallen for the king, but she'd also seen the signs that her time as lover was coming to an end. Unlike her predecessors, Alecine had prepared for the inevitable breakup by preparing a dossier of secrets that would have brought the king to his knees, records of payoffs to less-than-respectable individuals, under-the-table contracts for exorbitant quotes on construction projects that left royal accounts empty and Daxon's personal accounts full. When she'd given in to her anger and agony at being rejected for a younger woman, she'd threatened the king. A sympathetic maid had warned Alecine that the police were coming to arrest her and her family for treason. When Alecine had tried to withdraw money for their escape, she'd found their accounts frozen.

The slam of the door against the wall as Alecine had rushed into his family's home still woke him up some nights, her frantic cry of "Leo!" making his heart pound. His mother's sobs as she'd learned that her privileged life as wife of one of the most revered members of Linnaea's court was coming to an end still echoed, too. At the time it had terrified him even as he'd patted his mother's back, trying to tell her it would be okay. But now he looked on the memory with disgust for how quickly she'd abandoned him and his father, her hope that disassociating herself from the Adamas would help her salvage her own future more important than the man she had once gone against her family to marry.

Catapulted from the luxury of a wealthy household to the dirty, unforgiving streets of Europe, Cass, his father and Alecine had lived a harsh life that first year while his mother had returned to her family in France.

Grief hit so fast he barely masked it. He could still remember his mother walking out the front door with a Prada suitcase in hand, ignoring her husband's desperate pleas. She'd whirled around, told Cass he could come with her but would never be able to see his father again, not if they were to recover from the destruction Aunt Alecine had brought down upon them. He'd chosen to stay. She'd walked away without a backward glance. It had taken Cass nearly a month to stop crying himself to sleep.

"I was born in Linnaea. My family lived there for generations. My aunt had a falling-out with the king, your father. We were asked to leave."

Briony frowned. "That seems harsh. What did they fight about?"

"My father was the former treasurer. My aunt had strong views on how the government was spending money and made her opinions known. It turned ugly." His shrug masked the banked coals of a slow-burning anger that had been torturing him for nineteen years. Just like his significantly pared-down version of events was so sparse it bordered on a lie. "But political differences are a part of life. Your father is still not partial to my family. But things have changed drastically in the last few years."

"The country's on the verge of financial disaster."

"Done some reading?" he asked with a slight smile.

"A lot," she confessed. "I don't understand all

of it, but it sounds like they're steps away from a depression."

Somehow Daxon's public relations team had managed to cover the true reason for the country's situation. The king liked to spend money, regardless of the state of the country's finances. Rumors abounded, but few had proof.

Unlike Cass. Another incentive for Daxon to agree to his terms.

"They are. A marital alliance between Tulay and Linnaea will solidify their future."

Briony cocked an eyebrow. "Why can't you just give them the money?"

Cass chuckled. "It would certainly be easier if things worked that way. Have you heard of the term 'marriage of state'?"

Briony shook her head.

"It refers to a diplomatic marriage or union. Yes, I could just lend money to your father. But would you lend money to someone with no agreement? Consider this the same, but multiplied by billions of dollars."

"What do you get out of it?" She sat back and crossed her arms. "It sounds like other than marriage, you're just lending a bunch of money for nothing."

Your father loathes that I'm marrying into his family.

"Not nothing. My family and I are being reestablished into Linnaean society. While I'm being very generous with the terms of the loan, a five percent return on my investment over the next ten years will elevate my fortune even further. Trade agreements are being established between Linnaea and my adopted country, Tulay, agreements that would never happen without a union like ours."

She stared at him for a long moment. Valid reasons, all. But would she accept them? Or would she sense something else lurking beneath the surface?

"This is truly a strategic move for you?"

Danger lurked in her tone, anger and possibly even hurt. But he had no time for such emotions.

"Yes."

She blinked, then looked away. Tension settled between them. He continued to regard her with an unblinking gaze, waiting, biding his time. His patience was legendary.

"Stop staring."

"Why would I stop staring? You're beautiful."

Her lips twitched, a gesture he marked as a point in his favor.

"Let's not fight, Briony. You asked a question and I answered. We're on one of the most exclusive, luxurious private planes in the world. You should enjoy yourself."

Her fingers stroked up and down the leather armrest. His eyes followed the sensual movement for a heartbeat before he forced his gaze back to her face.

"I know I'm doing the right thing. For me. For them." Her shoulders sagged. "But it's hard not to have regrets. To wonder if I could have done something to prevent all this."

"With your stepfamily?"

She looked back out the window, the sun falling across her skin and highlighting the freckles on her nose.

"I hate his drinking."

Those words cost her, judging by the downward pull of her lips and the tensing of her shoulders. He already knew everything, from Trey's six-figure gambling debt to how Briony had been the only person present at her stepsisters' teacher conferences last month. From what he knew, Trey Smith was a failure. If the luxurious lifestyle he had to offer didn't persuade Briony to leave, the chance to escape the role of servant would.

"He didn't used to be like that."

"They rarely start out that way," he replied drily.

By Alecine's account, Daxon had been a generous benefactor and adoring suitor. He'd kept up his pretense with her longer than his previous lovers.

But inevitably, the mask had slipped and the monster had appeared.

"Trey was a decent stepfather," Briony said, a hint of defense hardening her voice. "He treated me well, especially since I wasn't really his daughter."

"After all he's done, you still defend him."

"He is…was family. You love family no matter what."

Cass swore in French. "Loving family isn't a requirement, especially when someone treats you the way he did. Your mother never should have married him if he didn't show himself capable of that."

Briony looked away. "Trey was more involved when they dated. He wanted to be what my mother wanted him to be. It wasn't until after they were married that he realized he couldn't. I heard him and my mom arguing about it once, so I told her things were better."

"To protect your mother?"

She nodded once. "I wanted her to have her fairy tale."

"What if her fairy tale didn't have to involve a Prince Charming? What if it meant her daughter was happy?"

Judging by Briony's wide eyes, the possibility had never occurred to her. Part of him wished he had left her stepfather in his decrepit house to drown himself in beer and debt.

"He should have treated you like his daughter, regardless of genetics, Briony. That is a failing on his part."

The tremulous smile she gave him warmed his chest.

"Thank you."

He leaned back in his seat, this time allowing silence to fill the space between them. Briony surprised him by not rushing to fill the gap with inane chatter. Instead, she focused on the scenery they were rushing over thirty thousand feet below.

His father, Leo, had taught him patience. Patience was a valuable asset that, despite their family's billions now, could not be bought and few possessed. Yet Briony's quiet dignity stirred him in a way that was both new and unsettling.

The plane shuddered. The captain's voice filled the cabin.

"Sir, we're experiencing some minor turbulence. Please fasten your seat belts."

Briony rode out the bout of shaking with a slight tightening of her lips and a firm grip on her armrests. Another point in her favor. The last woman he'd traveled with, an actress, had shrieked and afterward sought solace in his arms, big crocodile tears sliding down her face as she'd pressed her ample and barely covered bosom against his chest.

Once the turbulence abated, Cass leaned back in his seat.

"Do you have any other questions for me?"

"Where will we live?"

"Linnaea. We'll stay in Tulay for extended periods, and of course we can visit Kansas as often as you'd like, or anywhere else you'd like to go. But there's too much to be done, especially in these first few years, to be away for long."

"So we'll raise our children in Linnaea?" she asked softly.

An image flared in his mind of a little red-headed girl with brown eyes, or perhaps a little boy with eyes the same vivid green as his mother. He'd known children were in his future.

But knowing who their mother would be made the concept more real. And, he acknowledged as his eyes caressed Briony's face, more enticing. Briony had already proven herself to be a strong and patient woman. While she overindulged those two bratty stepsisters of hers, he had no doubt she would excel as a mother. And she had proven that she wouldn't abandon her family when things got rough.

"At least two."

"Truly?"

"Yes. That wasn't just a ploy to get you to say yes."

She nodded, but a frown still lurked on her face.

"What is it?"

"It's just…weird. Talking about this lifelong commitment so factually."

"More marriages would be successful if the parties involved approached it pragmatically."

A chuckle escaped her, but it wasn't a pleasant sound. It was resigned, bleak. He didn't like it on her. He reached over and, when she didn't pull away, took her hand in his. He savored the bloom of color in her cheeks as he wrapped his fingers around hers. Fortunately, she couldn't see the effect she had on him—the uptick in his pulse, the tightening of his muscles as he skimmed his thumb over the back of her hand.

"Ours is not, nor will it ever be, a love match. However," he continued on before she could object, "it can be a partnership. A union based on mutual respect, companionship and, eventually, a family."

He released her hand, a physical reminder to himself to not push too far. She was softening; that was the most important thing right now.

He pressed the button to summon a flight attendant.

"Two glasses of champagne and a bowl of strawberries, please." At Briony's quizzical look, he shot her a smile. "We're celebrating your first trip beyond the Midwest."

Most women of his past acquaintance would have giggled or thanked him in a physically demonstrative manner. Briony, however, rolled her eyes as she chuckled.

"I don't think I've ever had champagne before five o'clock."

"Then I'm happy to be your first." She didn't even bat an eye at the innuendo, just shook her head and stood.

"I'll be right back."

He stood, as manners dictated. Briony started

to walk past. The plane quaked again, then pitched to the right. Briony cried out as she tumbled into him. He anchored himself and wrapped his arms around her. The plane steadied a moment later.

"Apologies, Your Highnesses," the captain said over the speaker. "Should be clear sailing for a while now."

The speaker fell silent. The soft instrumental music still played in the background. The engines of the plane hummed in the background. But the loudest sound of all was the thudding of his pulse. It didn't just thunder in his ears; he could feel the rush of blood pumping through his veins, the awareness crackling across his skin as he held Briony in his arms once more.

Her scent curled around him, sandalwood mixed with something light and floral that conjured images of flowering trees and the brilliant blue skies of spring. His hand skimmed up her back, grazing the silky curls that tumbled down nearly to her waist. He wanted to bury his hands in her hair, inhale the scent of her as he trailed his lips up her neck—

"Cass?"

He blinked. Briony sucked in a shuddering breath as her chest rose and fell.

Damn it. He had nearly given in, all because of one accidental touch. If he let lust rule his decision-making, he would be just like his aunt, just like his father.

Don't give in.

He gently released her, returned her oblique stare without a word, then watched as she disappeared into the back of the plane. Moments later, Julie, one of the flight attendants, bustled out with a friendly smile, a bowl of bright red strawberries and two glasses of champagne. He nodded his thanks, his gaze affixed to the bubbles rising to the top of the golden liquid.

The genuine interest in his future bride was an unexpected and unwelcome conundrum. He had heard enough of what Daxon's wandering eye had done to Alecine and countless other women to know he would never indulge in an affair after he took his vows. What little Alecine had said on the subject over the years had been the driving force for his adding a fidelity clause to the marriage contract. His own liaisons up to this point had been indulgences for the sake of pleasure, always with the knowledge that one day he would be tied in matrimony to a faceless bride. Sex would be a part of that relationship. Heirs were needed.

But he hadn't anticipated that the brief fantasy he'd entertained in his week of being Cass Morgan would not only continue, but flare up into something he struggled to control.

Which left him at a crossroads, he acknowledged as Briony walked back out and sat across from him, her face turned away from him. He needed to stay objective when it came to his future wife. But he couldn't withdraw too much and risk her becoming dissatisfied with their arrangement. If he could keep himself under control, then he could woo her as he'd wooed countless other women without surrendering himself to dangerous emotions.

He raised his champagne flute. When she followed suit, he clinked his glass to hers.

"To new adventures."

She narrowed her gaze as she took as a cautious sip. "To the unknown."

CHAPTER SIX

CASS SPUN HER around an elegant ballroom, crystal chandeliers twinkling overhead. She laughed up at him as she savored the warm appreciation in his eyes.

But then the warmth faded, replaced by cold calculation. She started to pull away. But as she turned, Stacy and Ella confronted her, yelling about homework and dirty rooms and laundry. Trey stood behind them, belly bloated, eyes bloodshot and a can of beer dangling listlessly from his fingers...

Briony woke with a gasp. She blinked against the bright light filtering in through the plane's windows. The plane's engines hummed beneath her.

Cass. She was on Cass's plane flying toward a new country and a new life. Trey and the twins were behind her, in the past. It was as if every mile they flew farther away from Kansas, the more the scales fell from her eyes that had blinded her to how bad things had truly gotten. How long had she given her entire self, her whole identity, to the purpose of supporting her family? How long would she have gone on doing so if Cass hadn't shown up in her bar?

She brushed hair out of her face with trembling hands. She could picture the sneer on Trey's face the last time she'd seen him, smell the alcohol on his breath the numerous nights she'd dragged him to his bed. She could feel the heat of his tears soaking through her shirt when she'd held him as he'd cried for her mother. She could hear her own desperate pleas falling on deaf ears as she opened yet another statement from an on-line gambling site with Trey's increasing debts.

Other memories rushed through. Trey asking her to call him by his name, not "Papa" or "Dad." Trey giving her a pat on the back before he swooped Stacy and Ella up into a boisterous hug. Marie, quietly asking Trey to be more affectionate with Briony and Trey assuring her he just needed more time.

Loving family isn't a requirement.

Cass's words returned, circled around in her mind. At first, she'd been excited to love Trey and the twins, to have a complete family like the other kids at school. But then, as it had become apparent that she would be treated more like the daughter of a friend than an actual daughter, she'd continued to hold out that maybe, one day, she would do enough, be enough, to be loved in return.

It would never have been enough, she realized. There was truly nothing left for her in Kansas, a thought that should have been depressing but instead felt like the shackles of her own making were falling off, leaving her feeling lighter than she had in years. She turned, pulled up one of the window shades and looked out across fluffy white clouds hanging against a beautiful blue sky. She could almost believe it was a foretelling of what was to come. The chance to start anew, to make something of herself and support the recovery of a country.

And her father. He hadn't come to visit her personally, but he'd still come after her in his own way, still put in the effort to find out about her life and invited her to become a part of his. It was more than Trey had ever done for her.

"We're forty-five minutes out."

His voice slid over her body, husky and dark. It called to her, awoke something deep inside her and filled her with an intense longing.

Don't.

Cass had stated multiple times that love was off the table, that their relationship would be similar to what she'd known so far: an association built on what she could do for him. What he sparked inside her was physical. But beneath the burning desire that had slowly been building since he walked into her bar was something far more dangerous—emotion.

Forty-eight hours ago, she would have leaned into him, sought comfort from the man she was slowly falling for.

Except now she knew the truth. He didn't want her. Everything he did, from the champagne and strawberries to any other grand gestures, would have to be taken with a grain of salt. He didn't love her. Yet knowing that had almost been freeing. Unlike the one other serious relationship she'd been in and the handful of dates, there was no wondering, no questioning of where things were headed.

She turned from the window and met Cass's amber gaze.

"I'm excited to see Linnaea in person."

She kept her voice neutral, her attraction suppressed. There had been that one moment yesterday when she'd fallen into his arms after the unexpected bout of turbulence and she'd been clutched against him, certain—her traitorous body even hopeful—that he would kiss her. But the look of heat in his eyes had disappeared so quickly she must have imagined it or even projected her own foolish desire onto him. Aside from that one moment, he'd been noticeably less flirtatious and more businesslike, a stark contrast to their week of dancing around each other with veiled innuendos and seductive glances. She hadn't just been acting confident when she'd flirted with him. She'd *felt* confident, sexy, even beautiful.

Remember that, she reminded herself. Even if he had been acting, she hadn't. She had glimpsed a view of who she could be without the trappings of her narrow-minded family focus. She could be a confident, independent woman all on her own. Doubt trickled in. Some of her excitement was for the adventure ahead, of moving to a new country on the spur of the moment, of becoming involved in something bigger than herself. But a large part of her enthusiasm rested on meeting her father and brother. Was she still pinning too much of herself on family? She'd been picturing a beautiful reunion, the kind she saw in movies where the father looked at his long-lost child with tears in his eyes as he drew her into his arms. But what if it didn't turn out like that? What if her father was kind but distant, the way he'd been in his letter? What if her brother was resentful of her presence? Trey had once accused her of seeing the world through rose-colored glasses, of not accepting the bad with the good and putting people on a pedestal so high they couldn't help but fall off.

She swallowed hard. At the time his words had cut deep as he'd tied his biting remarks into a lecture on the boy she'd been seeing. But now... she was doing exactly that. Combining her fictional dreams of her birth father with the actual man himself and idealizing him before she even met him.

What if she hadn't left her former life for a better one? What if her father and brother rejected her and she was left alone in a foreign country tied for life to a man she barely knew? She wasn't just embarking on some grand adventure. She was getting married. For life.

The sun disappeared behind a cloud, and the interior of the plane darkened. The unease that had lingered beneath the surface since she'd made her decision returned with a vengeance and left her adrift once more, ensnared in a tangled mess of loneliness, doubt and exhaustion.

"I took the liberty of purchasing some clothing for your visit to the palace."

Cass's words yanked her out of the storm swirling around in her head. She forced a small smile.

"Jeans and T-shirt won't cut it for my first trip to see the king?"

His lips twitched. "Something more formal would be appropriate."

With a quick nod, she passed through the doorway into a bedroom. *His bedroom*, she realized as she glanced around the small space. A full-size bed occupied one side, covered in a vibrant red comforter. Three dresses were draped across it. Her mouth dropped open. She'd never seen such beautiful gowns in person. Each one was a work of art.

"Anna Vega."

She whirled to see Cass lounging in the doorway, hands in his pockets, a smug smile on his face that said he knew he had impressed her with his choices.

"Who?"

"Anna Vega. A very talented and sought-after designer."

Briony swallowed hard. The most expensive

thing she'd worn was a prom dress she and her mother had found at half price at a thrift store.

"So…expensive?"

Cass's face hardened. "Don't worry about the cost, Briony."

His casual dismissal of what she could only assume was an astronomical price irritated her.

"If I just wear my jeans and shirt, could I sell the dresses and pay off some of my family's debt without having to marry you?"

The words had barely left her lips before she regretted saying them. She was overreacting because of her own fears and self-doubt.

Cass's face sharpened into granite, his amber eyes so hard she couldn't help but shiver.

"I'm sorry," he said silkily as he advanced into the room. If she'd thought it an intimate space before, it was downright claustrophobic as his sensual presence filled every nook and cranny. She stepped back into the mirrored wall, the coolness of the glass belying the heat that traitorously flashed through her veins as he loomed over her. "Perhaps our memories differ as to what transpired yesterday. I don't recall forcing you to sign that contract."

"I didn't really have much of a choice," she retorted.

"You had choices, Briony." He leaned down, bracing one arm against the wall as he caged her in with his body. "Three of them, in fact. You chose to come to the airfield. You chose to get on my plane. And you chose to sign that contract."

White-hot anger warred with her awareness of just how close Cass was, how it would take just one slight move to press her mouth to his.

As if sensing her thoughts, his lips turned up into a cold, calculating smile.

"I know people better than they know themselves."

With that pronouncement hanging in the air between them, he leaned down and kissed her. It wasn't the sweet kiss she'd dreamed of back when he'd just been Cass Morgan. No, this was the kiss of a prince who was used to getting his way, a fierce kiss that assaulted her senses and made clear who was in charge. Despite the heat, he kept his hands on either side of her, not touching. A caress that lacked intimacy as he held himself back and kissed her on his terms.

All of the emotions from the past forty-eight hours swirled up inside her: anger, desire, hope, excitement, lust, fear. The fierce mix tore through her and propelled her up onto her toes. She wrapped her arms around his neck, returned the kiss with a fervor that surprised even herself as her fingers sank into the silky strands of his hair.

He froze for a moment. She didn't open her eyes, half terrified she'd see what she couldn't handle any more of: rejection.

Then a growl vibrated against her lips. The sound moved through her body, a hum of electricity that made her gasp. Cass's arms crushed her body to him as he took advantage of her parted lips to slip his tongue inside her mouth. Liquid heat pooled between her thighs. An ache started to pulse deep within her. Her hips arched against him, her hands tightening as she moaned.

One hand came up, fingers grazing the side of her breast, the touch burning through the thin cloth of her T-shirt. The ache shuddered, then spread through her veins like a wildfire she couldn't control. She wanted her shirt off, clothes off, his body pressed against hers, naked, hot, hard as he slid inside her and claimed her as his…

"Cass, please."

He stepped back so suddenly she nearly fell forward. He caught her arms, but as soon as she'd steadied herself, he moved away. Bewildered, she brushed her hair out of her face and looked at him. He stared back, his eyes glowing gold. He didn't bother to hide his deep breathing as his chest rose and fell, muscles outlined beneath the white material. Nor did he bother to hide the noticeable bulge between his thighs. Heat rushed into her cheeks as her gaze flickered back up to his...

...to see shock mirrored in his amber eyes for a brief second before he suddenly shut down, a mask dropping back over his face, the hint of Cass gone before she could blink and replaced with Prince Cassius, his breathing controlled once more. He was still handsome, still sexier than any man she'd ever met, but distant, regal.

Who was this man she was engaged to marry? Had the flirting, the seductive dance, the way he'd looked at her as if he couldn't bear not to touch her, all been true? The possibility that he was just affected as she was gave her some comfort.

"Cass—"

"That was careless of me."

Her mouth dropped open. "What?"

He stepped back and gestured toward the dresses. "Does one stand out to you?"

Her fingers curled into fists. "You know, my

mind is elsewhere right now. I'm a little confused."

He glanced at his watch. "We're now less than forty minutes out. You should choose."

"Maybe I don't like any of them."

"Wear one of the dresses or wear your jeans. It makes no matter to me."

Before she could summon a witty retort, he turned and walked out.

The door closed behind him. Good thing, too, because she had been an inch away from grabbing one of the books and hurling it at his obnoxious head.

She sucked in a steadying breath, one meant to refocus her attention as much as it banished some of the lingering heat from her body. So they were attracted to each other. Fine. People all around the world kissed and had sex and did all of sorts of things without putting their hearts on the line. She could, too.

She had to, if this was going to work.

She ran a frustrated hand through her hair. Did she even want it to work? Could she truly accept a loveless marriage?

Her phone vibrated in her pocket. She pulled it out to see an email from her bank. A quick glance revealed that it was just one of several that must have come through when she was sleeping. Credit card balances, zero. Mortgage balance, zero. Confirmation of two new accounts established in Stacy's and Ella's names, both with six-figure statements.

She slipped her phone back into her pocket. Whether she wanted it or not was beside the point. She would make it work.

She surveyed the gowns on the bed. Part of her wanted to stalk out of the bedroom in her jeans and shirt just to spite him. Except, she acknowledged irritably, the only person she would be hurting would be herself. With another deep, cleansing breath, she shoved the kiss into the deepest recess of memory and focused on the dresses that lay before her.

The first, a deep red that reminded her of the color of wine with a short-sleeved top and a full skirt and a ribbon about the waist, was beautiful but just a tad too formal for a simple meeting. The second was sky blue but was crafted of the most delicate-looking lace she'd ever seen, threads of silver holding the intricate pieces together. Stunning, but she would probably snag it on something before she left the plane.

The last dress, though, seemed perfect. The pale lavender bodice and waist were bedecked with small jewels. Formal, but the knee-length skirt and sleeveless top lent a casual flair that made her feel more at ease.

As she slid the dress on, she couldn't help but feel a small tingle of anticipation. In just a matter of hours, she would finally meet her father.

She focused on that and ignored the apprehension tightening the muscles in her neck.

CHAPTER SEVEN

THE CASTLE LOOKED as if it had been crafted from a fairy tale. A sparkling white palace stood against the backdrop of pine trees dusted with snow. Towering spires topped by crimson flags waved in the breeze. A cobblestoned drive wound its way in a serpentine pattern up the hillside. As the limo pulled up to a stunning marble staircase, Briony nervously smoothed the folds of her skirt.

She tore her gaze away to glance at Cass. He'd barely looked at her since she'd emerged from the bedroom dressed in her new finery. He'd murmured a "You look nice" before resuming his phone conversation. A limo had whisked them away from the airport around the outskirts of a quaint-looking city Cass had identified as the capital city, Eira. Two- and three-story buildings that looked as if they'd been crafted a couple centuries ago were interspersed with several more modern-looking towers.

With every passing mile, Cass's face had grown tense, his jaw hardening as his eyes sharpened. Was it difficult for him, being back in the country he had been torn from as a child?

An uncomfortable sensation settled in her stomach. Cass's story about his aunt and her father having a falling-out had been so vague. How could a simple disagreement over spending have led to the family being asked to leave the country? She should have pursued it more on the plane, but they'd transitioned so quickly to talking about Linnaea's financial problems that she'd forgotten.

Until now. The apprehension she'd suppressed on the plane, the feeling that she'd missed something in this rapid journey from lonely barmaid to secret princess, spread across her skin, a persistent itch she couldn't get rid of.

A guard opened her door. Cass kept a hold on her elbow, as if he were afraid she would bolt at any moment. Another guard escorted her and Cass up the stone stairs, through a set of double doors and into a stunning three-story hallway with soaring ceilings and walls covered in paintings that looked old and expensive.

It was beautiful, Briony acknowledged, but

cold, more like a museum than a home she could picture growing up in. How odd, too, that the palace would maintain such an extensive collection of art when the country was in such dire financial straits.

Stop judging. For all she knew, these paintings could have been in the palace for years, decades even, long before the recession.

A young woman with pale skin and equally pale blond hair pulled into a severe bun waited for them at the top of yet another sweeping staircase. She waited until a maid dressed in traditional black with a white apron had taken their coats and disappeared into the depths of the palace before she spoke to Cass.

"Your Highness," she said in a clipped tone, bowing her head just slightly enough to have it count.

"Clara. A pleasure to see you again."

The thinning of Clara's lips suggested she was anything but pleased to see Cass.

"I received your message thirty minutes ago, Your Highness." Her ice-blue eyes drifted to Briony. Something flashed in them before she turned back to Cass. "We didn't expect you until Monday. Had you notified the palace sooner, we would have been more prepared."

"And risk not giving the king a surprise?" Cass replied with a smile so cold it rivaled the ice in Clara's glare. "You know how much he loves surprises." He glanced over her shoulder. "Besides, Alaric is expecting me."

"Prince Alaric," Clara corrected stiffly.

Cass ignored her correction and turned to Briony. "Meet your half brother's right-hand woman, Clara Stephenson. The country would fall apart without her work."

Despite his mocking tone, Briony noted a thread of genuine admiration in his voice. Judging by Clara's frigid gaze, however, she didn't pick up on it.

Clara dropped into a shallow curtsy. "It's a pleasure to meet you, Your Highness," she said, her voice a tad warmer as she addressed Briony. "Your brother has been most anxious to meet you."

And what about my father?

Her earlier worries returned in full force.

"Thank you. It's nice to meet you, too."

"Clara," Cass broke in before either woman could say anything else, "would you give Briony a tour of the palace? Just a quick one, twenty minutes or so, and then bring her to Alaric's study?"

He ignored Clara's indignant huff and kept his gaze on Briony. His eyes gleamed. Cold tendrils of suspicion sank deeper into her skin.

"Cass, what's going on?"

He gently cupped her upper arms in a surprisingly intimate gesture.

"I'm speaking with King Daxon and Prince Alaric privately before I introduce you. Is Alaric in his office?" he asked as he released her and turned to Clara.

"*Prince* Alaric," Clara snapped, "and yes—"

"Excellent." Cass started to walk away.

"After I take you to—" Clara started to say.

"I know the way. Thank you."

Cass strode confidently down one side hallway without a backward glance. Clara stared daggers at his retreating back. But when her eyes flickered to Briony, she recognized the emotion lurking in the other woman's gaze.

Pity.

Cass's blood pounded through his veins as he neared Alaric's private office. Nineteen years. Nineteen long years of biding his time, of having plan after plan dashed, only to have his archnemesis himself hand him the key he needed to unlock both Linnaea's salvation and his family's vengeance.

He'd almost ruined it, too, with that damned slipup with Briony earlier. Kissing her on the plane had been a mistake, one that had shocked him at how quickly he'd succumbed to the surge of lust. Between his anger at her accusations and the unsated passion that had been building between them for a week, he'd acted on instinct. He'd seen the look on her face. She'd been just as affected as him, which was both incredibly sexy and very concerning. He couldn't let Briony think for even a second that they could have a relationship where their attraction ruled over common sense.

But then she'd walked out and she'd looked absolutely stunning, every inch a future princess. She had picked the lavender dress, a gown that had looked almost plain to him when he'd seen them laid out across the bed. But on Briony, with her vivid red curls and bare shoulders thrown back as if she owned the palace, she was mesmerizing. Who knew elegant could be so subtly sexy?

As the limo had drawn closer to the palace, the silence between them had filled the interior, thick and oppressive. For the first time since he'd begun his quest, he knew a moment of true doubt, not just the vague morality questions that he'd brushed aside. Linnaea was in trouble. He was ensuring a steady flow of money into the country, money he could oversee and ensure went to good use instead of a worthless real estate project or kickbacks to political cronies; it was the right thing to do.

And his aunt deserved to have her revenge against the man who had driven her and her family to the point of ruin.

But as he'd looked between the approaching palace and Briony, looking so strong and lovely and yet also lost among the cavernous backdrop of the grand hall he'd guided her to, he wondered if the cost of his success was too much.

He turned down another richly carpeted hallway, this one less cluttered with marble statues and priceless paintings than the others. While Daxon insisted on featuring his most costly purchases throughout the main wing seen most by the public, Alaric had managed to slowly but surely clear the hall that housed his office.

As a child, he'd never been in this part of the palace. When he'd first stepped foot in here a month ago, he'd been escorted between two armed guards. He could still see the smug, arrogant smile on Daxon's face when the tall wooden door had swung in and revealed the nephew of his former lover-turned-enemy.

How satisfying it had been to see conceit drain from the old mongrel's face when Cass had plonked not only copies of Aunt Alecine's documentation on the table, but a file on the long-lost princess of Linnaea.

He approached the same door and knocked once. For a moment, there was silence. Then the door swung open.

"Cassius."

Cass was tall, exceptionally so, but even Alaric stood above him by an inch or two. The heir to the Linnaean throne was a larger, more masculine version of his sire. Where Daxon's face had an almost delicate quality, Alaric's was made up of hard lines and a sharpness that had enhanced his reputation as a notoriously private yet fierce leader. Daxon had tied his son's hands on many matters. But the few things he did allow his son control over, Alaric took and ran with a leadership that even Cass grudgingly admired. If there was one thing Cass was certain of, it was that

Alaric hated Daxon almost as much as, if not more than, he did.

"Alaric."

Alaric's eyes, a similar emerald to that of his sister's, narrowed at the lack of formal address. Few people dared to push the buttons of a man who was rumored to be even colder than his father.

"Is she here?"

Cass nodded.

"Did she sign?"

Another nod. The tiniest quirk of Alaric's lips was the only indication that he was displeased.

"Then it's all going to your plan?"

Cass's mind conjured up the feel of Briony as she'd wrapped her lithe body around him, returned his punishing kiss with one of her own that had set his body on fire. He pushed it away, but another image replaced it; Briony, gazing out the window of the plane with hope on her face as they'd left Kansas behind. He would most definitely be able to offer her a better life. But he knew that a large part of the excitement that had sparkled in her eyes had been because of meeting her birth father.

The father he was about to introduce her to

who was far worse than the stepfamily she'd left behind.

You should have told her.

He could have still persuaded her. His plan to help her stepfamily, the chance to meet Alaric, all of it could have still been enough.

But now was not the time for regrets. And regret was just another gateway to feelings that needed to stay out of their arrangement.

"Yes. It's all going according to plan."

Clara glanced irritably at her watch for the fourth time as she walked Briony down yet another hall filled with paintings.

"The east wing hallway features—"

"Clara," Briony interrupted with what she hoped was a diplomatic smile, "I know Cass sprang this on you. You probably have better things to do than walking me around the palace. If you'll just take me to Prince Alaric's study, I'm sure it will be fine."

Clara frowned, but then cast a longing glance at her watch.

"I am quite busy today. We have an important series of events with the Swiss ambassador coming up in three weeks, and assuming…" Her voice trailed off.

"Assuming I marry Cass, a wedding to plan?" Briony asked with a self-deprecating grin.

A tiny smile cracked through Clara's smooth mask.

"Yes." She grimaced. "A week after Christmas."

"Then please don't worry about this tour. Cass has inconvenienced you enough."

Clara stared at her for a moment before she let out a surprised laugh that transformed her expression from dour to startlingly beautiful.

"May I be frank, Your Highness?"

"Of course. But only if you call me Briony."

Clara glanced around the empty hall. "In private, yes. In public, however, I must adhere to protocol."

"I understand."

"Briony, when your brother, Prince Alaric, told me that you would be getting married to Prince Cassius, I worried for you," Clara confided as she led Briony down another hallway.

"Worried for me?"

"He has a reputation."

Briony thought back to the numerous photos of Cass with models, actresses and other famous women on his arm at various events over the years. Something that felt too much like jealousy curled in her stomach.

"I'm aware. Although it seems like he's kept out of the news in recent months."

"It's not just his dating history." Clara guided them around a corner and up a flight of stairs. "The history between Prince Cassius's family and the Van Ambrose family is not a positive one."

"Cass mentioned something about that."

A look of relief crossed Clara's face. "I'm glad he told you. We were surprised when he offered the marital alliance. But it will be good for... Your Highness? Briony? Are you all right?"

It sounded like Clara's voice was coming from far away, a distant echo ringing in her ears. She put out a hand to brace herself against the wall.

Cass set all of this up.

The way he'd talked Friday night, she'd assumed Daxon had come to Cass. But as she reviewed the conversation, she realized that while Cass had certainly been clever with his phrasing, he hadn't explicitly said who had requested the alliance.

Betrayal turned her blood to ice. She knew Cass had used her, but she thought he'd at least been up-front with her. Instead, he'd orchestrated this entire play. To what benefit, she couldn't be sure, but based on what little he had shared, she had a pretty good guess.

"I'm fine," she said with a wan smile. "I think just all the travel and information overload, I'm a little dizzy."

"I'll get you some water." Clara guided Briony to a chair set in a small alcove. "We're just around the corner from Prince Alaric's study. Once you're feeling better, I'll take you to him."

Clara quickly walked off. Briony waited a heartbeat before she stood and walked down the hallway. She paused at the intersection of another hallway and then turned in the direction of murmured male voices. As she drew closer to a slightly cracked door, she heard Cass's distinct voice. Just the sound of his deep tones set off a conflicting mix of desire and disgust.

"...set a date yet?" she heard a man ask, his voice deep like Cass's but flat and lacking any trace of warmth.

"We haven't discussed it yet," Cass replied smoothly. "However, the contract stipulates within sixty days, which means eight weeks from yesterday."

"What about the money?" This voice sounded

much older, the raspy faintness reminding her of Trey after a night of binge drinking.

"It's all in the contract, Daxon." Cass's reply was much colder this time.

Daxon. It felt like someone reached into her chest, grabbed her lungs and squeezed. That had been her father's voice, infused with greed and disdain. Just the sound of it sent a chill skittering down her spine.

Her mind grasped at something, anything that might explain the coldness in Daxon's voice. Anything but the possibility that her birth father was just like the family she'd left behind, perhaps worse.

"You forget where you are, *Cassius.*" Despite the weakness in Daxon's voice, his tone was dangerous. "You are in the royal palace of Linnaea. You will address me as Your Majesty."

"I didn't realize Linnaean families stood on ceremony in private."

Daxon's cruel chuckle made her throat tighten as her heart twisted. "Marrying my bastard child doesn't wipe away the stain of your own pathetic lineage. You will never be family."

"Not by blood. But how does it feel to know the nephew of the woman you tried to destroy will officially be a prince of Linnaea?"

She closed her eyes against the hot sting of tears. Her fears on the plane paled in comparison to the awful truths she'd just overheard. Her fiancé had had an ulterior motive: revenge. And from the sound of it, her birth father was even worse than her stepfather.

What now?

The voices in the office dimmed to angry murmurs as she closed out the world. What did she do? Leave and find a way back to the States? And return to what? Cass had said he would pay for Trey's treatment, their debt and the girls' trust funds no matter what.

But then what? She didn't have any desire to go back. So where would she go? And if she backed out of the contract, what would happen to the people of Linnaea?

Cass's voice trickled out once more. Her heart gave a painful leap in her chest. Even after all of his betrayals, she couldn't help but mourn what could have been, what she'd glimpsed on the plane just hours ago.

Her eyes opened as she lifted her head. There would be time to make her decisions later. Determination dried her tears and stiffened her spine. Right now, she needed to confront the men who had turned her life upside down again.

She didn't bother with knocking, just pushed the door open and walked in, her shoes clicking on the hardwood. Three men turned to face her. Cass's lips thinned as he took in the sight of his fiancée. She barely spared him a glance before her gaze swung to the other two men in the room.

Despite his age, King Daxon Van Ambrose was still a formidable man. His shoulders were more stooped, his slender body thinner beneath his suit and his skin ashy. But his emerald eyes, so like her own, flickered with a cold, shrewd intelligence. The black hair she'd seen in the photographs of Daxon with her mother was gone, replaced by silver that gave him a distinguished air.

The resemblance between him and his son, Prince Alaric, was clear, though Alaric was taller, burlier and colder. His face must have been carved from a glacier it was so still as he regarded her with his own green gaze. Also, unlike his sire, his hair was a dark brown, cut short on the sides and slightly longer on the top.

Cass moved to her.

"You're early."

She ignored the question in his voice and gave him a brittle smile.

"I figured it was time to meet my family."

She was done adhering to his schedule, his way of doing things.

His eyes searched her face. She stared back at him, daring him to stop her. At last, he conceded with a brief nod.

"Of course. Briony, may I introduce King Daxon Van Ambrose and his son, Prince Alaric, of Linnaea."

She turned to face her father and brother. What should have been a joyous moment was instead one full of pain, fury and perhaps worst of all, embarrassment that she had allowed herself to be duped by their machinations and her own immature hope.

"Hello."

Daxon started forward. Had she not just heard him, she probably would have been fooled by the wide smile that stretched across his face and missed the cold calculation in his eyes.

"Briony. I'm so glad to finally meet you, my dear."

Briony stepped back out of reach of his embrace and held out her hand.

"Glad I can be of service, Dad."

CHAPTER EIGHT

BRIONY STOOD ON the balcony of her private suite. The sun had already started to sink behind the snow-capped peak of the mountains in the distance. Her room overlooked the palace grounds and the hundreds of acres of forest to the west. A stunning view fit for a princess.

As was the suite Clara had led her to after her brief meeting with Daxon and Alaric. Daxon had stared at her after she'd delivered her stinging line. Alaric had stepped in and shaken her hand, introducing himself before suggesting she be shown to her suite.

"It's been a long journey," he'd said firmly as he'd steered Briony to the door. "Rest would probably be best before we talk."

Clara had appeared a moment later. Briony hadn't been able to stop herself from glancing back at Cass. For once, there had been no smug smile or hint of danger in his gaze. No, he'd looked almost regretful. She'd wanted to lash out at him, to grab the contract from his hands and rip it right in two. But she wasn't going to give him the satisfaction of seeing her fall apart.

She sighed. Cass had made no pretenses about their marriage being anything other than a contracted alliance. But she'd at least thought his intentions had been somewhat noble. To find out that he was motivated just as much by a personal vendetta as he was supposedly saving the people of Linnaea left her feeling...

Empty. Hopeless. That brief, beautiful burst of confidence and independence on the plane seemed light-years away. Her own father had used her, too. Even after hearing the words from his own lips, part of her wanted to cling to the illusion that it had all been a terrible misunderstanding. That she hadn't just left the only world she'd known to be confronted with yet another person who just wanted to use her. Remembering the sound of his voice, the disgust in his tone when he'd said "bastard child," made her sick to her stomach.

It wasn't just hopelessness. No, it was also regret that she had ever pined for a man like Daxon. If what she'd overheard was any indication, her mother had been right to run.

The regret burned brighter, tightened her

throat. How many years had she wasted wishing for a dad when she'd had a mother who had loved her?

Pretty far down the road of self-pity, she thought with a disgusted sigh as she shivered in the winter cold and glanced over her shoulder. Her suite was a vision of royal luxury. A rounded bed dominated one side, raised up on a dais with a peaceful painting of the mountains on the wall. It was covered by violet silk sheets and a thick white comforter. Marble steps led down to a sitting area comprising a red fainting couch and matching chairs done up in velvet and trimmed in silver. Wood roared in a stone fireplace, flanked on either side by bookcases set into the.

Poor little rich girl. She'd heard the sentiment often enough, had done her fair share of eye-rolling when she'd read an interview with the latest actress or model who talked about the hard parts of their lives, the lack of privacy, the pervasive loneliness.

Except now she understood it all too well.

The door swung open. Her eyes narrowed even as her heartbeat sped up at the sight of Cass standing in the doorway. Clad only in his dark trousers and midnight-blue shirt, sleeves rolled up to reveal his tan forearms, he looked sinfully good.

She turned her back to him. How could the man be so manipulative and still look so handsome?

The door to the balcony clicked open.

"Cold out here."

The shiver that traveled down her spine had nothing to do with the freezing winter air tugging at her hair.

She gritted her teeth. Just because her body found Cass physically attractive didn't mean the man wasn't a manipulative snake.

"Matches the personalities of most of the people who live here."

The door shut. She felt him come up behind her, tensed, anticipated...

Nothing. He was waiting to see what she would do. She raised her chin. Two could play at that game. And she'd been letting him call the shots. Time to give Prince Cassius Morgan Adama a taste of his own medicine.

She couldn't say how long they stood out there on the balcony. The sun continued to sink behind the mountains, leaving behind peaks that glowed a dazzling array of oranges, reds and yellows. Overhead, the stars started to wink.

The wind picked up. She imagined the shooshing as the breeze darted in and out of the pine trees below, dislodging a bit of snow here or kicking up flurries there. If she focused on those details, it helped her forget the man standing less than a foot away.

"I've only said sorry once in my life."

Briony snorted. "I'm surprised you've said it even once."

Cass moved at her back, then circled around. His shoulder brushed hers as he came up to the railing and leaned forward. If the freezing temperatures bothered him, he gave no indication as he propped his forearms on the cold stone and gazed out over the landscape.

"It was when I found my aunt crying in the corner of the bedroom she, my father and I all shared." He breathed in deeply. "She blamed herself for getting us banished from Linnaea, for my mother leaving. She couldn't stop crying. She said love had destroyed not only her but her family. So I patted her on the back and told her I was sorry."

"Sorry for what?"

"Sorry for not standing up to the king. Sorry for not being the man I was supposed to be when she needed someone."

Briony's mouth dropped open in shock.

"How old were you?" she finally asked.

"Eleven."

She closed her eyes against the sudden pain as she imagined a young Cass, dark-haired with an innocent amber gaze, trying desperately to comfort his aunt.

"What did she say?"

"Told me it wasn't my fault." He looked away. "But it didn't matter. I felt like I had failed my family."

"Did…did my father force your family into that situation?"

She opened her eyes to see Cass regarding her with an opaque gaze.

"I don't know everything that transpired between my aunt and your father," he said finally. "I do know they were lovers. I know she threatened him toward the end of their relationship. And I know he in turn threatened her with prison for treason, as well as anyone who chose to stand with her over him."

Briony's hands curled around the cold marble railing as queasiness overtook her. She'd heard plenty to confirm Daxon's true character. But hearing more evidence of her father's cruelty was almost more than she could stomach.

"I'm sorry."

"You have nothing to be sorry for," Cass said, his voice firm. "I don't blame you or Alaric in any way."

"Did my…did Daxon know what happened to you?"

"I doubt he knew or cared. He only cared about getting rid of her and slandering her to the point that no one would believe any stories she might tell about his nefarious activities."

His words to her father replayed in her head: *How does it feel to know the nephew of the woman you tried to destroy will officially be a prince of Linnaea?*

"So marrying me…it was never about Linnaea, was it? Just revenge."

"Do you think so little of me?"

His voice was steady. But his eyes were a mix of regal hardness and a hint of sorrow, a combination that seeped past her defenses straight into her bones. Part of her wanted to reach out and lay a comforting hand on his shoulder. But she couldn't just let go of everything he'd done: the deception, the subterfuge, the manipulation.

"Revenge can make good people do bad things."

He stared at her for a long moment before he

stretched out his hand. "Would you come with me? There's something I want to show you."

"What?"

He sighed. "Will you trust me? One more time?"

Was she a fool to even consider saying yes? What could he possibly show her that would make any of this okay?

"Please, Briony."

Whether it was the "please" or the way he uttered her name in that deep, velvety voice of his, she couldn't say. Her rational mind screamed at her to say no, to demand that he rip up their engagement contract and take her home. Her body, however, had other ideas because her gloved hand slowly came up. Cass seized it in his before she could change her mind.

"We're going for a drive."

Ten minutes later, Cass steered the little black car he'd taken from the palace's motor pool off the lantern-lined lane of one of Eira's fashionable districts and onto a narrow street. He kept both hands on the wheel, his eyes focused on the increasingly pitted road and off the woman in the seat next to him.

When Briony had taken his hand, he released

the breath he'd been holding. Seeing the look of betrayal on her face when she'd walked into Alaric's office, watching how cold she'd become as she'd processed what she'd heard, had bothered him more than he cared to admit.

He'd expected Briony to seek him out after she'd been shown to her rooms. But as the minutes had ticked by, he'd found himself pacing, checking his phone and watching the door every time he heard footsteps in the hall. Finally, fed up with his own lack of self-control and a morbid need to find out what Briony was thinking, he'd stalked through the halls to her room.

Yes, he hadn't been entirely honest with her. Yes, he'd had ulterior motives. But it wasn't just about revenge. He needed her to understand why. Otherwise, he might as well tear up the contract right now because there was no chance in hell she would walk down the aisle to be wedded to him.

He brought the car to a stop at the edge of an attractive square ringed on all three sides by white town houses with green shutters. The fourth side contained a strip of shops and cafés, from a small bookstore to an art gallery. In the middle lay a park with swings and a few benches. With the light of the lanterns casting a golden glow on the snow, it looked like a post-card. Daxon might have been a selfish bastard, but when it came to image, the man knew how to make an impact.

"Only one row of those town houses is occupied." He felt more than saw Briony turn to look at him, but he kept his gaze focused on the buildings. "Van Ambrose Tower, the latest high-rise, only has twenty percent of its offices filled."

He pressed on the gas and kept driving. A few blocks later, the elegant town houses gave way to brick apartments smooshed together. The farther he drove, the more decrepit the buildings became. Gone were the fashionable black lanterns and cobblestoned streets. Here the roads were made of simple asphalt, cracked and in desperate need of repair. The few streetlights that were working cast only weak pockets of light on streets choked with refuse. Underneath one cracked light, a teenager dug in a trash can.

"This is what I want to fix, Briony. I did not lie to you about that. Eira has at least some fashionable districts that cater to the few wealthy families left and the smattering of tourists that come through. But the rest of the country lives like this. The internet, social media—all of it's kept under lock and key to hide what's going on beyond the capital. The only reason I knew all these years is because my father still has friends here who managed to get letters out that it continued to get worse after our banishment."

He turned down another street, one filled with old houses. He parked in front of a two-story brick home that, despite its crumbling exterior and weed-choked yard, still clung to some of its old glamour. Double doors with stained glass guarded the entrance. Even though a rock had been thrown through one long ago, the craftsmanship was still evident.

"I used to stare at the floor in the morning and watch the sun come through the doors," he said quietly. "There were so many colors."

In the darkness, Briony shifted.

"For the longest time, I dreamed of coming back here, of raising my own children in the house I grew up in." He nodded to the other once-elegant homes now sagging under the weight of abandonment and disrepair. "That dream is gone. The houses have been condemned, and the entire street will be razed in the spring." He turned and speared her with his gaze. He needed her to understand. "But progress can still be made, Briony."

For a moment, all he could make out was her

profile; the slight curve of her nose, the graceful line of her jaw. Even in the dim light of the streetlight, her red hair glowed.

"You lied to me."

"I did not lie. However," he interjected as her head snapped about and her lips parted, "I won't deny that I could have handled things better. I provided only the vaguest details about my family's history with yours."

"What happened? What did my father do that made all of this deception worth it?"

Cass's hands tightened on the wheel. "He broke apart my family."

For a moment the only sounds were the distant wail of a siren and his own heartbeat. It was the first time he had spoken the words out loud. He didn't look at Briony, couldn't if he was going to finally share what had happened.

"My aunt was his mistress. I imagine not long after your mother fled."

The rest of the story came tumbling out. How his father's position as assistant to the minister of the treasury had given him access to documents on how King Daxon's frivolous spending was plunging the country into economic chaos, information he had shared with his sister, Alecine. How Alecine had used that information and other intelligence she'd gathered to threaten Daxon when he'd tried to dismiss her for his next lover. And how Daxon had retaliated by telling Alecine she had twenty-four hours to leave with her family and never return or be thrown in prison for treason.

"He froze our finances. Slandered our name to anyone who would listen and made it impossible for my aunt and father to find work."

"What about your mother?" Briony asked softly.

"My mother chose to return to her family in France." His knuckles turned almost as white as the snow on the ground as his fingers wrapped even tighter around the leather. "She knew the struggles we would face with no money and Daxon's vitriol following us throughout Europe. She preferred the comfort and ease her family could offer."

"And they didn't offer to take you in, too?"

"They did. If I agreed to never see my father again."

Briony's gasp sounded like a gunshot inside the car.

"How awful."

"My mother was furious with my aunt, and angry with my father for siding with Aunt Alecine. She told him he could go to Daxon, pledge his loyalty and turn my aunt in to keep us safe and keep our standing in society. But Father refused."

"Family duty," Briony murmured softly.

"Family honor," Cass corrected. "My father and aunt had plenty. My mother had none."

"So you fled."

"We fled. We made our way to Rome. It took a year for us to climb out of the little hovel of an apartment we lived in. My father and aunt crafted new identities for themselves, worked whatever jobs they could find to slowly build their way back up while trying to stay under the radar in case Daxon caught wind of where we were and changed his mind about coming after us." The gingham hanging over the cracked window flashed in his mind. "One night my aunt came home with this red gingham tablecloth. She hung it over a window that had cracked when some boys threw rocks at our window. Every time she tried to hang it, wind would come through the crack and blow it down. She finally started to cry and kept telling me over and over how sorry she was." He could still see her face, eyes puffy as tears ran down her cheeks. "She told me how she wished she could have stood up to Daxon and saved my father and me from everything."

"So you decided one day you would stand up to Daxon for her."

Cass's head snapped around as he faced Briony, surprised that she had so quickly seized on the moment he'd decided to get revenge.

"Yes."

"Cass, you were eleven," she said quietly. "That was too much to take on."

"It wasn't. My father lost my mother, a woman he had loved and who, when she was younger, loved him enough to defy her family and marry him when he was just a lowly lawyer versus the trust-fund prince they had picked out for her. My mother made her own choices," he acknowledged, "but without Daxon's labeling my aunt and father traitors, their marriage wouldn't have ended."

"You don't know that," Briony argued. "A woman who would leave her husband when he needed her the most could have left for any number of other reasons later on in life."

"But she didn't," Cass ground out. "She left because Daxon threatened to throw my aunt in prison for treason, as well as anyone who aligned with her."

"And your father chose your aunt."

"Not over my mother." Cass's voice vibrated with anger. "She accused him of the same thing. But he knew it was only a matter of time before our family would be targeted, too. It wasn't just choosing to support his sister. He was the first one to mention to my aunt that he had found some troubling inaccuracies in some financial documents. My aunt is smart, very smart, when it comes to finances. Her relationship with Daxon was turning ugly. So she started compiling evidence." A vein began to throb in his neck. "My aunt lost her whole life. She lost everything, as did my father, and no one bothered to stand up to a tyrant."

Briony didn't back down from his anger. She just continued to watch him with those eyes so like his oppressor's, yet so different. Where Daxon's were hard, flinty chips of green, Briony's were warm and vibrant, a window into her soul.

"Obviously your aunt had a change in fortune, at least."

A quick smile flashed. "My aunt made her way up from cleaning bathrooms in a hotel to working as a blackjack dealer in the hotel's casino. One night she dealt cards for the reigning prince of Tulay, Daniel Callas. She beat him every hand that first night. He came back every night for a week, then proposed on his last night in Rome."

"That sounds romantic."

"More like the result of loneliness. Daniel was a widower. He married my aunt because he liked her and she didn't kowtow to him. The papers termed it a 'whirlwind courtship,' dug up her past with your father and labeled her a crown-seeking gold digger. But after a year of making significant improvements in everything from Tulay's tourism industry to housing reform, the rumors faded and the people embraced her."

"And you became a billionaire."

He shrugged. "Not without help. Daniel sent me to university. He placed me in charge of one of his holdings, a shipping company. I invested the money I made, diversified into real estate, tourism and transportation. My investments paid off. I told myself one day I would return to Linnaea and offer your father a loan to rebuild the country."

"From what little I overheard this evening, I take it accepting a loan from someone related to his former mistress who almost destroyed him angered him?"

"Enraged is more like it," said Cass with a

small smile. "But Daxon is not without his pride, either. I knew that just the financial offer, even though almost no one else would be willing to put so much money on the line with the country's economic history, would not be enough to sway him."

"But I was." Briony's voice was small, shock and understanding as the last piece of the puzzle fell into place.

"Yes. Daxon has made no secret about his reputation as a womanizer. But aside from getting photographed with his date of the month on his arm, he's kept most of the sordid details private. He'd made no secret that aside from Alaric, he didn't want any more children. For an illegitimate child to be revealed, and for it to be known that he had done nothing to support that child once he found out about its existence, would have been a death sentence for him publicly. He's sick. From what the doctors say, he has less than a year to live. He knows his legacy as a leader is in tatters. The financial offer, combined with his chance to be seen as righting the wrongs of his past and doing right by his child, were more important than rejecting me. Marital alliances still serve a purpose in many parts of the world, and it acts as insurance that Daxon won't back out."

"And you have your revenge by being the sole savior of Linnaea, getting your family's banishment reversed and marrying into the very family that rejected you."

Briony's voice was flat, her face emotionless. Coldness swept through Cass. He had had those almost exact same thoughts. But when stated out loud, they sounded truly heartless.

Briony frowned. "But why did Daxon not have Alaric marry someone for financial support, or even Daxon himself get married?"

"Alaric has been engaged to some heiress for years. I don't know the details, only that every attempt he's made to finalize the marriage has been rebuffed. I don't think he has high hopes for it ever happening, but he's trapped by a contract. As for Daxon, his reputation is so well-known in the right circles that no woman with the financial resources he needs would agree to a marriage with him."

"Leaving you as the only savior in sight." One corner of her mouth twisted up into half of a sardonic smile. "And here you are."

"And here I am." He released the steering

wheel and spread his hands out. "That's the whole sordid story."

She tilted her head to the side. "Was what my father did worth the lies?"

Anger spiked. "Did you not just hear what I told you he did? How he tore apart my family? And how, exactly did I lie? I told you that night at the Ledge exactly what the marriage contract would entail."

"Yes, you offered to marry me in exchange for giving money to the country." Briony's eyes flashed with anger. "But you also insinuated that my father wanted to see me knowing full well he didn't care about my existence. You lied to me. And," she said as she held up a hand to stop his reply, "don't say you didn't outright lie. You deliberately misled me. That counts as a lie."

He couldn't have picked a better future wife if he'd tried. Briony didn't capitulate, didn't back down. She was too fierce, too determined. A far cry from his own mother, who had turned weak at the first sign of not having a luxurious life.

And if he didn't own up to his mistakes now, he would be no better than her. No better than Daxon, even, who had lied and manipulated his entire life.

That thought stopped him cold. When had he

become so blind, so focused on fulfilling his sense of duty to his family and his revenge that he ignored the tactics he'd used to achieve his goals?

He looked at Briony, truly looked at her, for the first time since their kiss on the plane. She was backed against the door of the car, not out of fear, but to put as much distance between them. A woman who had come from almost nothing, left behind her entire life for the promise of something better, a promise he had falsely portrayed.

"Make that three."

She frowned. "Three what?"

"Three times in my life I've apologized. I'm sorry, Briony. I did lie." He hated saying the words out loud, hated himself in that moment for who he had become. "I lied and I used you. Just like your stepfather, your stepsisters and your birth father."

She stared at him for so long he wondered if she would ever say anything. If she said nothing, if she made a scene and demanded he fly her back to the States or anywhere else in the world, it would be no less than he deserved. He should have been honest, should have stuck to what he could do for her and her family instead of adding the spin of being reunited with a father who wanted nothing to do with her.

At last, she sighed.

"I'm still angry with you. But no, Cass, you're not as bad as my family. Especially," she added with disgust dripping from her tone, "not as bad as my *father*."

"While I'm pleased to hear that, how did you arrive at that conclusion?"

"Aside from not telling me who you were at first and suggesting my father wanted to see me, you've been up-front about everything else. Especially about your expectations for our marriage."

"I never wanted to lie about that," he said firmly. "But you can help me help this country. You can help me help your brother. I can help your stepfamily. And we can still have a pleasant life together."

Silence descended once more. Briony stared at him for a long moment before she turned to look at his childhood home. He glanced at the front porch. He'd spent hours on the porch swing with his father, listened in rapt attention to his father's stories about what had happened at work, took pride in his father's hard work at helping the country take steps to become stronger.

Cass looked away. That time was past.

"I want children. So do you. They'll want for nothing."

"What about love?"

The words were spoken so softly he almost didn't hear them.

"What about it?" he asked. Hadn't she just heard him?

"Will you love your children?" She pinned him with a bleak gaze effused with a sorrow so deep he almost had to look away. "Or will you be like my stepfather and withhold the one thing they need?"

He barely swallowed his anger. She had a right to ask.

"Romantic love is off the table for me. But loving one's children…that's another matter entirely. I will love any children you bring into this world."

He'd expected something more from her, a smile or some other confirmation. But she merely nodded and looked back at the house. The seconds ticked by, each one longer than the last, as he waited for her answer.

"All right."

He hadn't expected excitement. But neither had he expected to hear her sounding so listless.

"All right?"

"All right," she repeated softly as she leaned her head back against the car seat and closed her eyes. "Will you take me back now?"

The rest of the car ride was spent in utter silence. Briony didn't open her eyes until he pulled the car back into the garage beneath the palace. He had barely put the car in Park before she had unbuckled her seat belt and gotten out. He swore under his breath and got out. She'd almost made it to the elevator.

"Briony."

She paused, shoulders rigid, hands balled into fists. Slowly, she turned but kept her head down, that curtain of red obscuring most of her face.

"I am sorry. For hurting you."

Then she turned and disappeared inside the elevator. The doors swished shut, leaving Cass alone in the garage.

He didn't know how long he stared at the closed doors. When had his perfectly laid plans, his years of plotting, become more important than his honor? When had his revenge become more important than his true duty, using his wealth to support Linnaea's recovery?

Marrying Briony was still a crucial part of the plan. A marital alliance would cement relations between Linnaea and Tulay. It would also make it much harder for Daxon to renege on their agreement.

As long as he could refocus his attention where it belonged and rein in his complicated emotions for his future wife.

CHAPTER NINE

BRIONY STARED AT her reflection in the mirror. She didn't look like herself. Her hair had been straightened, the waist of her white cap-sleeved dress cinched with an emerald belt that matched the petticoat peeking out from beneath the knee-length skirt. Matching green earrings sparkled at her ears.

She sucked in a deep breath. The cosmetologist Clara had ushered inside her room just after dawn had managed to conceal the deep shadows beneath her eyes. She had crawled underneath the thick, warm blanket and silk sheets of her king-size bed...and mourned. Mourned the death of the dream she'd held on to as a girl of who her father was. She'd envisioned him a hero, a firefighter, perhaps, or an adventurer, an astronaut who looked down on the planet on one of his trips to the space station and wondered where his daughter was.

Fanciful. Foolish.

She'd heard those adjectives from Trey often enough. Unfortunately, she was proving him right more times than she cared to admit.

By the time she'd woken up that morning, her grief had morphed into anger. Anger at the powers that be that had bestowed upon her an unloving stepfather and an even more unloving birth father. Anger at Daxon for being such a callous brute. Even knowing his diagnosis didn't alter her feelings. Just a day ago, hearing that her birth father would most likely not see next Christmas would have made her world tilt on its axis.

But last night, her world had simply shuddered for a moment. She didn't wish death on anyone. But it was hard to summon more than a vague remorse for a life cut short. Not when she had not only witnessed his cruel nature but heard about how he had treated everyone in his life, from a former lover to a child whose family had been ripped apart.

Cass had lied to her. But, she acknowledged grudgingly as she smoothed a wrinkle out of her skirt, unlike anyone else in her life, he'd come clean. He'd apologized, twice. And he'd stuck to his original offer. How many men would have continued to lie, would have manipulated her even further to get what they wanted? How many would have tried to play up a love angle, even tried to seduce her to secure what they wanted?

It didn't excuse what he'd done. But it did let her know that despite his mistakes, her original evaluation of his character had been accurate. He was a good man trying to do the right thing both for the country he remembered and loved and for his family.

Could she be strong enough to enter into a loveless marriage? Even if it was for the greater good?

But, she reminded herself, *that still didn't explain the kiss*. He'd emphasized the professional nature of their relationship multiple times. Could he remain so detached when it came to making heirs? Just the thought of his body pressed against hers, heated skin growing hotter still as they explored each other, made her breath catch.

Fanciful. Foolish.

She yanked on the zipper of her dress and groaned when it snagged on her bra. That's what she got for fantasizing. She should have let Clara stay to help her with the dress.

A knock on the door had her hurrying to the door.

"Oh, Clara, thank good—"

She came up hard against a solid wall of muscle. She stumbled back, her legs becoming tangled in the voluminous folds of the petticoat. An arm wrapped around her waist and hauled her against a very strong body. A spicy, woodsy scent wrapped around her.

"Where's the fire?"

She tilted her chin up to look into Cass's eyes. His teasing smirk disappeared as his hand moved up and came to rest on her bare back.

"Uh…my zipper got stuck."

His fingers drifted down, lightly skimming over her skin and setting every nerve ending on fire until he reached the zipper.

"Turn around."

Was it just her imagination or did his voice sound husky? She followed his order and turned, catching sight of her reflection in the mirror across the room. His black hair and tan skin stood out against the white of her dress, his broad shoulders dwarfing her frame.

With a deft twist, he freed the zipper and slid it the rest of the way up.

"Thank you."

"You're welcome."

He stepped back as she turned around.

"You're going to give other European royals a run for their money on the best-dressed list."

A different type of warmth suffused her body, pleasant and cozy at his compliment and admiring gaze.

"Thank you. Clara picked it out." She surveyed his impeccable gray suit and navy tie. "You look good, too."

His lips twitched. "Thanks."

She wrapped her arms around her waist. "So what are you doing here?"

"The conference starts in forty-five minutes. Clara will have a heart attack if we're not there at least thirty minutes ahead of time."

He rattled off the remainder of the schedule as Briony grabbed her coat and gloves off the bed: the conference, followed by a carriage ride through the streets that would take them to lunch with members of the Linnaean government. She shrugged into her coat as she swallowed hard.

She'd said yes last night because she'd wanted to break free of her past, to stop doing things for her family and start looking to the future. She had the chance to do something with her life, not just for her but for a whole country.

Except she hadn't thought too much about appearing in the public eye until now.

"Briony."

She looked up to see Cass watching her with an opaque gaze, his handsome face smooth.

"If you've changed your mind—"

"No," she interrupted. "It's not that. It's just the thought of being on display in front of all those people." She swallowed hard. "What if I make a mistake?"

Cass's lips tilted up into a full-blown smile as he chuckled, a rich, warm sound that calmed some of the nerves fluttering around inside her chest.

"You will make mistakes, Briony. But don't forget that yesterday you stood in front of your birth father, who's also a king, and essentially told him you weren't falling for any of his lies."

He closed the distance between them and captured one of her hands in his, bringing it up to his lips. The kiss he brushed across her fingers wasn't the seductive caress he'd bestowed upon her in the Ledge. It didn't make the touch any less provocative.

"You are a worthy princess, Briony. More worthy of the title than any other woman I've met."

Her chest constricted at his words and the admiration in his caramel eyes. It was just as intoxicating, if not more so, than the attraction between them.

"Cass—"

"Your Highnesses!" Clara appeared in the doorway, tablet in one hand, cell phone in the other. "Are you ready? It takes approximately ten minutes to reach the front of the palace from this wing."

Briony looked back at Cass, but his face had smoothed once more as he turned to face Alaric's right-hand woman.

"Of course, Clara. I admire your attention to detail."

Clara snorted. "I'm sure." Her gaze slid to Briony and she actually smiled, her eyes softening. "You look beautiful, Princess Briony. If I may be so bold, Your Highness," she said to Cass, "you're very fortunate."

Cass acknowledged the comment with a nod but said nothing as he held out his arm to Briony. She accepted it and kept her gaze averted. If she was going to make their arranged relationship successful at all, she needed to put distance between the two of them now. She'd done it fairly well last night, and that had been after a transatlantic flight and numerous heart-wrenching revelations. She could do it again.

She had to if she was going to survive the choice she'd made with her heart intact.

Cass glanced at Briony out of the corner of his eye as she leaned over to better hear what Linnaea's minister of the treasury was saying. A smile crossed her face, and she laughed. Judging by the smitten look on the minister's face, he was as besotted with Briony as the rest of the people she'd met.

He'd wondered for a moment if Briony was going to be able to handle the day. She'd kept her head down on the elevator ride from her wing to the main floor. She hadn't said a word on the walk to the front of the palace. And when it had been time to step out onto the main staircase landing where the press conference was being held, Briony had stopped, her face pale.

But before he'd been able to swoop in and rescue her with a platitude, she'd inhaled deeply, squared her shoulders and walked out, one hand laid elegantly on his arm.

She'd handled the conference like a pro. Clara had avoided giving her anything to say in public, but she'd smiled at the press and gathered crowds with a genuine sweetness he knew would reflect well in tomorrow's papers. That she had stopped to accept a flower from a little girl and given her a hug on their way to the carriage had made an entire country fall in love in the span of a heartbeat.

It had also made his earlier admiration flare into a fierce pride. His fiancée was a strong woman who was poised to become an exceptional leader.

Unfortunately, his esteem had opened the gateway for his suppressed attraction to also flame up. The carriage ride to the hotel had been pure hell. They'd sat next to each other, the cold winter day making the heat of her leg pressed against his even more intense.

And now he was experiencing...jealousy. Ever since they'd been escorted into the hotel's ballroom, there had been a nonstop parade of people walking up to be introduced to Briony and congratulate her on her engagement, welcome her to Linnaea or, for a few calculating individuals, attempts to try to ferret out details about Briony's lineage.

Briony handled it all like she'd been doing this for years.

The spotlight being focused on her had given him plenty of time to observe. Unfortunately, it also gave him plenty of time to think. He'd gone up to her suite to ensure she hadn't changed her mind before the conference. He hadn't expected to find her looking so stunningly beautiful. And he most certainly had not anticipated a mere graze of his fingers on bare skin would make his muscles lock up as he fought the thundering pound of his pulse demanding that he slide the zipper not up but down, baring her body for him and him alone to see.

Now that everything was official and Briony had been introduced to the public, now that she wore an emerald engagement ring on her finger and there were no immediate obstacles to their impending marriage, he was faced with the growing conundrum of his attraction to his fiancée.

If it was just simple sexual interest, that would be easy, even welcome. But the problem that had developed with Briony and didn't show any signs of letting up was the strength of his attraction and how it had become interwoven with the emotions that surged forth no matter how much he tried to stifle them.

Why had he shown Briony his family's house? He had seen shock, compassion, even begrudging acceptance of what their union could do for the people of Linnaea when he'd shown her the trash-ridden slums of Eira's seedier underbelly. There had been no need to bare one of the most painful parts of his life.

But he had. A compulsion had seized him, a burning need for her to see him not as a spoiled prince wanting to get his own way, but as a man who had a duty to fulfill.

So why? That question had haunted him all night. Perhaps it had been the betrayal in her eyes when she'd walked into the study and confronted him, Daxon and Alaric. Or maybe it had been seeing the coldness she'd wielded like a shield last night, a stark contrast to her usual warmth.

Daxon approached, dressed in an impeccably tailored dark green suit with a light brown tie and brown shoes. He shook hands and smiled along the way. But his gaze stayed laser-focused on Briony.

Cass's hackles rose as he stood and intercepted the king.

"Daxon," he said with a smile for the cameras even as he gripped the older man's hand in a tight grip. "What do you want?"

"I want to see my daughter," Daxon replied with his own smile, clapping Cass on the back like they were old friends even as he winced under the pressure of Cass's fingers.

"Your daughter?" Cass chuckled and leaned down so that no one else could hear. "Don't you mean your bargaining chip?"

Daxon's mask slipped a moment as his thin lips stretched into a taut line.

"You're the one who proposed this, Cassius. You backed us into a corner."

"You backed your entire country into a corner with your irresponsible spending—"

"Gentlemen."

Both men turned to see Briony smiling at them with worry in her eyes.

"What's going on? People are starting to look this way," she said quietly as she slipped her hand into the crook of Cass's elbow as if they'd been touching each other intimately for months.

"A reporter has asked for a photo of the two of us, but your fiancé has decided I'm not allowed to be around you," Daxon said stiffly. "I don't recall seeing that in the contract."

Briony glanced up at Cass.

"You have enough going on today," he replied in a low voice, ignoring Daxon's snort. "I didn't want him to add more stress."

Something softened in her eyes, an appreciation that suddenly made him feel like a conquering warrior.

"Thank you." She squeezed his arm. "I can handle him."

As she walked away, Cass watched them for a long moment before he slowly sat back down. If today was any indicator, Briony truly didn't need him. She would be more than capable of handling her royal duties and living a life separate from his aside from duties that required their joint presence or the raising of their children.

It was what he had wanted, what he had been concerned she couldn't handle. So why, when presented with evidence that he was getting everything he had hoped for and more, was he feeling so bereft, like he'd just lost something incredible?

This was why emotions were better left out of arrangements like this, he thought crossly. They screwed everything up.

CHAPTER TEN

BRIONY WALKED THROUGH what in the spring would no doubt be an incredible rose garden. The bushes had been expertly trimmed back, the remaining branches now covered in a light layer of snow. But the trellises that ran between the elegant stone pillars evoked images of flowers bursting into bloom and creating a walkway lined on either side by the most beautifully colored roses. Come late spring, this would probably be one of her favorite places.

It was thoughts like those that kept her going on days like today. That and, she thought with a small smile as she glanced over her shoulder at the sled trailing behind her, simple joys.

The week since the press conference had flown by. Every morning she'd awoken, eaten in her room and then joined Alaric for a brief meeting in his study at his invitation. She'd been pleasantly surprised to find him a warmer person when he wasn't around their father. Perhaps one day, they could even be friends.

Daxon, on the other hand, had shown no interest, a blessing given how just the sight of him made her stomach tighten in disgust. The few times she saw him, he greeted her with a brisk nod. If others were around, he would pat her on the back or press a cool kiss to her cheek. She tolerated those brief interactions, but she ensured they were brief. By unspoken agreement, they each had acknowledged that they wanted nothing to do with the other outside the necessary public engagements.

As the days passed, the anger that had manifested that night after her drive with Cass had dimmed. Perhaps it was because she'd spent so many years wishing things could be different with Trey that she accepted the reality of her situation quicker. Or perhaps it was because Daxon was so far from the idealized father she had built up in her head that it was easier to distance herself from the cold, vain man he was revealing himself to be. She wasn't completely over his rejection or her own disappointment. There had still been moments of pain throughout the week. There would be more to come, of that she had no doubt.

But she was stronger than she had been. And, she thought with a smile, she finally had something to focus on besides family or the relationships that would never be. Something that was hers and hers alone.

During one of her morning meetings with Alaric, she'd shared what she wanted to focus on as a princess of Linnaea: restoring the country's education system. Alaric had been surprisingly supportive of her ideas, which is why the last few days had been consumed with setting up a council of former teachers, administrators and other professionals who could use their experience to start rebuilding Linnaea's schools.

It had been thrilling to throw herself into something she loved, to exchange ideas and have a goal to focus on. It also kept her mind off her fiancé.

Her footsteps fell harder as she moved off the path and tromped through the deeper drifts of snow, each stomp of her boots an effort to drive his face from her memory. The next round of royal events would start this weekend, kicking off with a visit to a hospital and ending with a gala exhibition of a new museum in Eira. She'd only seeing him in passing or at dinner with Alaric. They were polite, formal and barely spoke. After their encounter in her suite with the zipper and his moment of chivalry in trying to protect her from Daxon, he'd withdrawn once more into the chilly, distant prince who had emerged after their kiss on the plane.

Unfortunately, their distance didn't stop her body from responding to his presence. The low rumble of his voice rippled through her veins. A glimpse of his slow smile at dinner made her heart beat faster. The insightful questions he asked about the work she was doing reminded her of the blissful week of ignorance she'd spent flirting with Cass Morgan.

She'd known when she'd signed the contract that she was signing away her chance to love and be loved by the man she'd give herself to. A fact she'd struggled with after clinging to that idea for so long.

Yet after seeing how her vision of meeting her birth father had gone up in flames, what was the point in dwelling on what she used to want? Unfortunately, letting go of the past had resulted in even more lurid dreams of what it would be like when they finally explored the passion that had been simmering between them since the moment he'd walked into her bar.

Enough of that.

She traipsed up a hill behind the palace and stopped at the top. She sucked in a deep breath of crisp, cold air before she sat in the toboggan, planted her gloved hands in the snow and pushed off.

The sled flew down the hill, skimming so fast the wintry landscape flew by. She threw back her head and laughed as the sled reached the bottom and continued for quite a distance across the flat plain that stretched for what seemed like miles before giving way to the forest in the distance.

At last, the sled came to a stop. She sat there for a moment, then slowly rolled off the sled into the embrace of the cold snow. She wiggled around a bit, then spread out her arms and legs and swept them up and down. When had she last made a snow angel? At least a couple of years, maybe even more.

Her movements slowed as she gazed up at the crystal-blue sky. The meetings and endless to-dos of royal life, not to mention the never-ending questions Clara peppered her with about the wedding, all faded away to the simple pleasures of playing in the snow.

A noise registered. She paused, listened, then

heard it again: a distant shout. Slowly she sat up in time to see a figure racing down the hill. As the figure drew nearer, it turned from a dark blur of arms and legs into the tall frame of a man dressed in a black winter coat with a matching head of equally black hair.

Cass.

"Briony!"

She started to push herself up out of the snow, but Cass was at her side faster than she had anticipated.

"Don't move," Cass ordered as he knelt down next to her. "Lie back. If you fell, you could have injured something."

"I didn't—"

"I'll call the medical team and—"

"Cassius!"

Cass blinked and stared at her as if no one in the world had raised their voice to him before. No one probably had, she thought grumpily.

"I'm fine. I went sledding, I rolled off and I made a snow angel." She gestured to the imprint behind her. "See?"

Cass let out a harsh breath and scrubbed a gloved hand over his face. "I saw you lying on the ground and thought…" He shook his head.

"I'm fine," she said again, but gentled her voice. "I can take care of myself."

"I'm fully aware that."

Was he irritated with her? Before she could question his cryptic remark, he grabbed her hands and pulled her to her feet.

"Regardless of whether your tumble in the snow was intentional or not, you shouldn't lie in the snow for too long. You could get frostbite."

She rolled her eyes as she picked up the rope attached to the toboggan and started trekking back toward the hill.

"I did grow up on the prairies of Kansas. I'm well aware of frostbite."

Cass didn't respond, but fell into step beside her. For a moment they walked in silence, the crunch of their boots in the snow surprisingly pleasant given the tension between them.

"Why did you come out here?" Briony finally asked.

"I went to your suite to confirm tomorrow's plans. The maid said you had decided to go sledding behind the rose garden."

"And you couldn't have confirmed the plans by text?"

Cass shrugged. "I've been up to my ears in financial statements and planning committees all week. I figured a walk would do me some good."

He reached down and grabbed the rope from her as they started up the hill, towing the sled behind him. Briony rolled her eyes again.

"Does your sense of duty and honor apply to pulling sleds?"

He surprised her with a small chuckle. "Perhaps."

A question rose to her lips, but she bit it back. Despite his overbearing attitude and need to protect, the walk itself was pleasant. She didn't want to ruin the first alone time they'd had in over a week.

"Something's on your mind."

Startled, she glanced over at him.

"When you're thinking about something but not sure you want to say it out loud, you get this little crease between your eyebrows and bite down on your lower lip."

She laughed. "I didn't realize I was that transparent. But yes, you're right. I was just wondering if sometimes you focus too much on your sense of duty and not enough on your life."

For several long moments, Cass said nothing. Briony inwardly cursed. Yes, she was engaged to the man and yes, they'd shared an intense, soul-stirring kiss. But that didn't give her the right to pry into the man's personal life. Not when their engagement was based entirely on business.

"What makes you ask that?" Cass finally asked as they neared the top of the hill.

"It's just that here you've been focusing on getting revenge and getting your family's banishment rescinded. You've accomplished that. But the few times I've seen you, you don't seem very happy."

Cass stared ahead as they reached the top, then turned to look back over the plain.

"I'm not."

She stared at him. She hadn't expected an answer to her question, much less an honest one.

"Why?"

"At first I thought it was the letdown that comes after something you've been anticipating or working toward for a long time. Almost like the aftermath of a holiday or celebration. But now..." His voice trailed off as he stared at the trees in the distance, his dark profile standing out in stark contrast to the pale walls of the palace behind him. "Most of my life has focused on achieving revenge against Daxon. The night I came back to Linnaea and was brought before your father, I felt powerful. It was as if that moment in the apartment in Rome when I felt so helpless and cowardly and the moment I stood before him merged. I righted the wrongs done to my family and I stood up to an oppressor." He turned to look at her. "Except there was nothing after that. I had focused so much on that moment that not even restoring Linnaea had become a focus. That anticlimactic emptiness has only grown since I acknowledged how I've treated you."

Briony reached out and laid a tentative hand on his arm. "I forgive you, Cass. It wasn't the best way to go about things, but I know your heart was in the right place."

Cass shrugged her hand off and stepped back. "Don't."

"Don't what?"

"Don't make excuses for me," Cass snarled. "My heart was focused solely on making your father feel backed into a corner, to make him feel the way my aunt did and as if he had no choice left but to do what I said." He leaned in, his eyes no longer golden but dark and hard. "I wanted to bring you before him so that he could be reminded every day that he had messed up. Your very existence damages his pride."

Each word landed like a punch to the stomach. But Briony didn't back down. She went toe to toe with him.

"And how about now?" she challenged. "Or are you just so determined to keep me at arm's length that you're telling me all this?"

"I'm telling you because it's the truth," he snapped back.

"Yes, but you're missing the other half of the truth!" she cried. Dear God, could the man be any more pigheaded? "You apologized. You told me everything. You offered me choices."

"I never should have put you in that position in the first place."

"No, you shouldn't have," she agreed. "But everyone makes mistakes, Cass. It's how we react to the people we've hurt with those mistakes and how we respond moving forward that matters. From what I've seen, Daxon is stuck in an endless loop of selfishness. Agreeing to the contract was more about his own pride than saving the country he hurt. My stepfather and stepsisters cared more about wallowing in their own grief than overcoming our loss as a family. I'm working on accepting that it's not me who's to blame for any of it. They are who they are— self-absorbed people who don't bother to look beyond themselves." She poked him in the chest. "But you aren't like that!"

Cass met her gaze, his jaw tense, eyes blazing. The tension in the air between them crackled, shifted from anger to that electrifying intensity that always seemed to be just out of reach.

Please kiss me again.

Cass jerked back as if she'd spoken the words out loud.

"You have a good heart, Briony. But you make far too many excuses for the people who hurt you."

He started to walk off. She blew out a frustrated breath.

"You know what I think the other part of your problem is?" she called after him. "You're a stuffed shirt."

Cass's steps faltered, then stopped. She watched his shoulders rise up toward his ears then fall. Had she said too much?

No, she told herself. *You never say enough.*

Slowly, he turned.

"A stuffed what?"

"A stuffed shirt."

He frowned. "Is that like a stuffed bird?"

Briony groaned. "No. It's an expression. It means formal, boring, pompous."

A glower darkened his face as he took a step in her direction.

"I can assure you no one has described me as boring."

"You spent how many years focused on getting revenge? And then once you have it, all you do is feel guilty for achieving what you've been working on for so long and attend meetings. What else do you want out of your life, Cass? When are you going to start living?"

Would it be rude to dig out her cell phone and snap a picture of the thunderstruck expression on his face?

"This coming from the woman who spent six months being a servant to her abusive family?"

She raised her chin, determined not to let him see how much the cruel but accurate comment hurt.

"And I made a choice to get away from that. What are you doing?"

"I'm working to make this country a better place."

"If you count reviewing financial statements and talking with committees as fun, then you're missing out." She gestured toward the sled. "When's the last time you went sledding?"

"When I was six."

Her mouth dropped open. "When you were six?"

"Yes."

"Okay, you want to prove you're not a stuffed shirt?" She knocked her boot against the sled. "Then go sledding."

"No."

"Ah, I see." She turned her back on him and swung one leg over the toboggan. "You're scared."

"You're not teasing me into going sledding."

"It's okay if you're scared. I won't tell anyone," she said as she looked over her shoulder and winked at his thunderous face before turning around to grab the rope. "But I still think—"

Her words ended on a squeak as a solid wall of warmth pressed against her back. A moment later Cass's legs caged her in on the sled, his arms wrapped around her to snatch the rope from her hands. She sat straight up, but a quick tug sent her falling back against his chest.

"All right, Briony," he murmured in her ear, sending a careening ache through her body that made her thighs tighten as her core grew hot. "Let's go sledding."

Before she could retort, he pushed off. Their combined weight elevated them to speeds she hadn't been able to achieve on her own. She laughed as they whipped down the hillside, savoring the rush of the sled, the icy air, the contrasting warmth of the man who cradled her so firmly yet so gently against his incredible body.

They reached the flat plain, the sled continuing to churn across the snow.

Until the sled hit something concealed beneath the snow. One moment Briony was cocooned safely in Cass's arms. The next she was sailing into the air, her body propelled forward by the momentum of their crash. A second later she hit the snow with a gasp. Cass followed a moment later, his muscular frame landing directly on top of her.

"Briony!" Cass lifted himself up on his forearms, one hand brushing the hair out of her eyes. "Briony, are you all right…"

His voice trailed off, and he frowned as she started laughing.

"I've never gone that fast before!"

"Your idea of living is very different from mine."

Briony's laugh died as the weight of Cass's body registered. The blanket of snow softened the world around them, making her more acutely aware of the pounding of her heart as Cass's eyes darkened.

"Have you thought about what it will be like between us?"

His question made heat bloom across her skin, the roughness of his voice sinking deep inside her and making her restless. She wanted to tell him no, wanted to say making love had never even crossed her mind.

But it would be a lie.

"Yes," she whispered.

Slowly, he lowered his head. She gasped as her gaze met his, amber eyes flashing with desire as he drew closer. Her eyes drifted shut just before his lips touched her.

I'm in trouble.

The fleeting thought disappeared as Cass kissed her with a slow, smoldering intensity. The contact made her gasp and arch into his body as she wound her arms around his neck. His lips left hers, moved over her cheek in a caress as light as butterfly wings, then down her neck. He placed an open-mouthed kiss at the base of her throat that made her moan his name.

Even if there was never any love between them, at least she would have this, a passion she'd never known was possible.

His hand found the zipper of her coat and pulled it down. The cold air kissed her chest, enhancing the heat of his touch. When his lips kissed the swell of her breast revealed by the parted fabric, she moaned.

"Cass!"

He stopped.

"Cass?" She opened her eyes as he lifted his head.

"If I don't stop now, I'll pick you up, carry you into the palace to my rooms and..." He leaned down and grazed another kiss across her lips, lightning fast. "I won't stop."

She swallowed hard. She wanted him, wanted him more than she had ever wanted anyone.

But if she went to bed with Cass, if she made herself vulnerable to him in any way, she would be surrendering her control. She'd risked, and suffered, rejection over and over again, from Trey and her stepsisters to Daxon. Was taking this step worth the risk? Not to mention she would be truly closing the door on the possibility of having her first time be with a man who loved her.

The thought stopped her cold.

Something flickered in Cass's eyes. Before she could gather her thoughts or reply, he pushed himself off her, then held out a hand.

She accepted it, allowed him to pull her to her

feet. Before she could say anything he turned, grabbed the rope of the sled and started off toward the castle.

Wait!

Her heart cried out, urging her to stop him. But the sight of his retreating back stopped the words in her throat. She had been about to make a split-second decision based on emotion. Cass had told her multiple times emotion had no place in their upcoming marriage.

She couldn't say how long she stood watching Cass walk across the plain. He stopped at the base of the hill, arched a brow and nodded toward the castle. Slowly, she followed. When she reached his side, they walked up the hill together. Once they reached the rose garden, he broke off and headed toward the stables without another word.

Once in her room, she drew herself a scalding bath. When she eased her body into the Jacuzzi tub, she imagined the hot water burning away all traces of Cass's touch from her skin.

Eventually they would have to be intimate. They both wanted children. But she had several years before she would be ready for a family of her own. Perhaps it would be better to postpone any intimacies until they'd gotten to know each other better.

Because if just a kiss was an indication of how quickly she could fall under the spell of physical passion, she needed time to fortify herself.

She would not risk losing her heart to her husband.

CHAPTER ELEVEN

CASS WATCHED BRIONY out of the corner of his eye as she surveyed a painting on the gallery wall. His fingers tightened on his champagne glass as his gaze drifted over the dark green gown, laced and fitted to her slender body like a glove.

He took a sip of his drink and grimaced as the bubbles hit his tongue. Where was a good whiskey when you needed one?

The last week had been perfect. He'd only seen Briony in public settings, in the dining room or Alaric's office. He had kept all temptation off the table. He'd focused on his committees, on working with Alaric to distribute funds, and had kept his interactions with his fiancée professional and brief.

Until he'd screwed it up. Again.

When she'd challenged him to go sledding, he'd been raw inside, not thinking straight when he'd decided to show her that he wasn't a stuffed shirt or whatever idiom she'd used. The moment he'd sat down behind her, felt her incredible body relax against him, heard her sparkling laugh as they'd raced down the hillside, he'd felt more alive than he had in years.

And then he'd landed on top of her, she'd whispered "Yes…" and the world had exploded. He hadn't been able to stop touching her, kissing her, tasting her. If they had been somewhere private and not surrounded by snow, he wouldn't have been able to stop himself from stripping her naked and sliding inside her incredible body.

His eyes narrowed as he watched Briony walk over to another painting, her head tilted to one side. It was better that he had walked away, for both their sakes. His past sexual encounters had been enjoyable. But no woman had inspired such lust in him. Before they had sex— *not made love*—he would have to find a way to tamp down the physical passion he felt for Briony. He wanted to enjoy his marriage, yes.

But too much of such raging intensity could lead into territory he wanted no part of.

Out of the corner of his eye, he saw Briony drift toward an open door with a sign above that read Artistes Linnaea. Her strong, confident movements were offset by the voluminous skirts, which gave her the appearance of gliding into the gallery. Her red curls had been wound into an intricate updo on top of her head, baring her neck to his gaze.

For a moment, he entertained the notion of loosening his self-control just a bit, allowing himself to embrace some of the feelings Briony inspired.

But like a well-tuned weapon, the image of Aunt Alecine sprang to mind, her shoulders shaking as she cried into her hands and told him over and over again that she was sorry for ever being stupid enough to fall in love.

As he took another sip of champagne and steeled himself to rejoin his fiancée, his aunt's sobs echoed in his mind, each remembered cry strengthening his resolve to not make the same mistake.

She couldn't take her eyes off the painting in front of her. A dirt road meandered through fields of golden grain. In the distance, against purple-blue mountains and trees tinged red, the palace of Linnaea stood tall and proud. A little girl stood off to the side, hair tossed in the wind as she kept one arm wrapped around the neck of a brown dog.

"What do you think?"

She turned to see a thin man, sporting round spectacles and a nervous smile. Dressed in a faded but clean collared shirt and dark pants, he looked out of place among the sea of costly clothes and jewels worn by the other guests.

She liked him immediately.

"It's beautiful. I was never good at art, but this is spectacular. And unlike some of the other art here, I can…" She paused, searching for the right words. "I don't know, it's like I can feel the painting. Feel the wind, the autumn chill."

The man flushed as his smile grew. "That's so good to hear."

She returned his smile. "I'm assuming you're the artist?"

"Hugo Verne, ma'am. Yes, it's my first work to be hung anywhere other than my living room or a local fair."

"You certainly earned it." She glanced back at the painting. "Is the little girl your daughter?"

His flush deepened with pleasure. "*Oui*, my daughter, Lorraine. She spends a lot more time with me at home since the school closed."

"I'm so sorry. Not having a school must be hard."

Sadness crossed Hugo's face.

"Most of the schools outside Eira closed within the last few years. We were told it was too expensive to operate."

The uncomfortable sensation that had settled in Briony's stomach when she'd walked into the museum and seen the opulent spending on everything from the mahogany floors to the white marble columns burst into full-blown anger. What had Daxon been thinking with constructing something this grand when the country couldn't even offer schooling?

"I'm so sorry."

"It's not your fault, ma'am. It could be worse."

"Still, something's being done."

Hugo's expression brightened a little. "I'm a little more hopeful after I heard about the marriage between King Daxon's daughter and a prince. I wasn't able to come into the city last week, but I've heard wonderful things about her."

Briony's stomach twisted. Hearing firsthand from someone outside the palace that marrying Cass actually had the power to enact change was both gratifying and terrifying. Gratifying in that, after so many of years of drifting through life without purpose, she had the power to do something. Terrifying because if she failed, she would always remember the hopeful light in Hugo's eyes and the painting of a little girl with her arm wrapped around her dog.

She sipped on her drink before she answered.

"I hope the marriage makes things better for everyone."

Hugo nodded eagerly. "I'm sure there will be some positive changes." He leaned in, dropping his voice to a conspirator's whisper. "I just hope she isn't like King Daxon. The man likes to spend money."

Briony chuckled. "I've heard she's nothing like him."

Awareness pricked the back of her neck. Without turning, she knew Cass had entered the room.

"Ah, Princess Briony." Cass's deep voice echoed in the cavernous room. "Admiring the local talent?"

Hugo's mouth dropped open before he clapped it shut and bowed so quickly at the waist Briony feared he would snap in half.

"Prince Cassius, may I introduce Hugo Verne,

the artist behind this beautiful watercolor," Briony said as she turned to greet her fiancé.

Dear Lord, he's handsome. Dressed in a tuxedo cut perfectly for his muscular frame, midnight-black hair combed back to show the carved architecture of his face, just laying eyes on him after less than thirty minutes apart made her heart beat faster.

Cass stopped next to her and observed the poor painter with an arched brow.

"Your Highness," he gasped, "I beg your forgiveness, I meant no disrespect, I just—"

"Hugo," Briony broke in as she grasped his hand and gently urged him to straighten, "you're fine. I'm still getting used to all this royal business anyway."

"But...but I insulted—"

"On the subject of how money is spent in this country, you and I are in total agreement," Briony said with a reassuring smile. "And on that note, my suite is unfortunately bare. Do you have any other paintings of the Linnaean countryside I could purchase?"

Hugo's mouth dropped open again. "You want...my painting...in the *palace*?"

"Yes, please."

"Of—of course! I can't believe..." His voice

trailed off, and he ran a hand through this pale hair. "How shall I…?"

"Why don't you stop by the palace tomorrow afternoon? I'd love to see more pictures of your work and learn more about what the education needs are in Linnaea. The council I'm assembling has a lot of experience to offer, but I'd enjoy hearing firsthand from parents."

She felt Cass tense beside her, but she ignored him.

"Yes, Your Highness," Hugo gushed.

"Now that that's settled, Hugo, how about you go grab yourself a glass of champagne before you keel over," Cass suggested.

"I will, sir. I mean, Your Highness. Your Highnesses," Hugo stuttered before he gave them both another bow and departed the room, excitement vibrating off his skeleton-thin frame.

"You've already managed to snag one fan, it appears."

Briony shot Cass a teasing glance. "Do I detect jealousy, sir?"

"From a starving artist who could barely talk to you once he realized who you were? Not likely."

"Unfortunately 'starving' sounds all too accurate," Briony murmured as she resumed studying the painting.

She started when Cass laid a hand on her waist. But then slowly she relaxed, allowing herself to enjoy the small contact and draw strength from his touch.

"He told you about his daughter's school."

She nodded. "He did. I knew they'd closed from the members of the council. But hearing it from a parent who was affected..." Her voice trailed off as she looked up at the carvings crisscrossing the ceiling, the elegant chandelier in the next room. "What on earth was Daxon thinking?"

"I don't think he was."

Before she could question him further, a small group of people entered the gallery. They curtsied and congratulated Briony and Cass on their engagement. More people filled the room as they realized the long-lost princess of Linnaea was inside. Questions started to fly, everything from whether Briony had really been a bartender to queries on the wedding.

"Thank you for coming tonight," Cass finally said diplomatically, raising his voice just enough to command the attention of the room. Briony watched as he took control of the crowd. The sensation in her chest when he stepped into the role of confident leader had nothing to do with physical desire and everything to do with admiration.

"After a long day, you'll understand if I escort the princess back to the palace," Cass finished with a winning smile.

He snaked an arm around Briony's waist and navigated through the crowds. They paused near a beautiful silver sculpture of a tree. Briony inhaled deeply before taking the last sip of her drink.

"That doesn't look like champagne."

Briony shot Cass a smug grin. "Brandy old-fashioned."

"Where did you get that?"

"It helps to get acquainted with the bartender."

Cass huffed. "Next time, perhaps you would be so courteous as to get me one, too, so I'm not drinking this sparkling stuff."

She rolled her eyes and held out her glass. She'd expected him to take it. But instead, he cupped her hand in his and brought the glass to his lips, keeping his eyes trained on her as he drank. Her heart hammered in her chest. The intimacy of the act left her breathless.

"That tastes very good," Cass murmured as he released his grip.

"Um...yes...yes, it does."

This time he didn't put an arm around her waist as they continued on through the museum. But he did stay close, whispering the names of dignitaries and members of the Linnaean parliament in her ear as they came up to meet her and congratulate her on the engagement. Each subtle murmur of support calmed some of her nervousness. She was much more at ease conversing with someone like Hugo than the well-dressed masses before her.

"You're doing great."

Cass's whisper made her spine straighten as her smile widened. His encouragement and support sent a much-needed jolt of confidence through her veins. She was, she realized, enjoying her time with him, despite feeling like a fish out of water among the gilded crowd of Linnaea's upper crust.

Perhaps Cass was right, she thought with a small, relieved smile. Perhaps she could enjoy her marriage.

At last, they reached the grand entrance.

"Ready to go home?"

A small smile tugged at Briony's lips. Even

though she still got turned around fairly regularly in the palace's corridors, the upstairs hallway that housed the royal family, the family dining room and the library had quickly become familiar and comforting to her. It was nice to have a home again.

"Yes."

Cass's gaze lingered on her for a moment before he helped her into her snow-white coat. He grabbed her hand and guided her down the red carpeted steps out into the snowy night.

Briony barely registered the crowd rushing at her before a light bulb went off in her face.

"Princess Briony, how do you feel about the closure of the hospital in Levrouz?"

"Did you know about the shutdown of the rural schools?"

"Do you think art is more important than paying the wages of national employees?"

The questions flew at her like barbed arrows, each one landing with a piercing blow. Shame washed over her as she looked down to blink the light from her eyes and saw the skirt of her dress. The dress that most likely cost thousands of dollars. How many people could that have helped?

Cass swore beside her before he stepped protectively between her and the photographers and reporters.

"Go back inside," he ordered over his shoulder.

"I'm not leaving you alone to deal with this," Briony retorted. "Can't I say something to—"

Her words were cut off as one of the ropes keeping the crowd back gave way. People surged forward, pushing past the overwhelmed security guards lining the aisle in their zest to get up close and personal with the mysterious princess. She took a step back, one heel catching in the voluminous folds of her skirt. Her arms pinwheeled in the air as she fell backward. A moment later she fell against the stairs, a startled cry escaping her lips.

A horrified silence descended on the crowd. Cass whirled around and knelt down next to her.

"Briony," he breathed, his voice strained. "God, Briony, stay still."

A flashbulb went off. Cass started to turn, murderous intent gleaming in his eyes, but Briony put a hand on his arm.

"Don't." Slowly, she sat up, wincing at the pain in her back. "I didn't hit too hard, and I didn't even hit my head."

"You're seeing a doctor when we get back to the palace," Cass said firmly.

Briony held her tongue. Arguing in front of reporters armed with cameras was not the best strategy.

More security guards poured out of the museum and pushed the crowds back. Cass scooped Briony up into his arms, stalked down the aisle and set her gently in the back of the limo waiting for them. He circled around, gave the driver a terse order in French as he got inside and then turned his attention back to Briony.

"You're certain you didn't hit your head?"

"Yes, I'm sure. Stop treating me like a child."

Cass's face was grim. "I never would have escorted you out the front had I known that would happen."

"But you didn't know, so stop blaming yourself."

"You still have a lot to learn about me, Briony." He leaned closer, his fingers sliding into her hair as he gently felt the back of her head. Her eyes drifted shut as she savored the feel of his touch.

"Such as?"

"Such as when I make a mistake, I ensure it's corrected."

Her eyes flew open.

"What do you mean?" she asked warily.

Cass's smile flashed white in the darkness of the limo.

"It means that until the palace doctor gives you a clean bill of health, I won't be leaving your side tonight."

CHAPTER TWELVE

CASS CAST ANOTHER glance toward the closed door of the bathroom. After the palace doctor had given her a thorough physical examination and pronounced her healthy aside from a few bruises, she'd told Cass she was going to take a hot bath.

That had been over an hour ago.

Where had his legendary patience disappeared to? He wanted to check on her, make sure she was okay not just physically but also emotionally. Being attacked by reporters in such a callous manner couldn't have been easy.

The door to the bathroom creaked open. Briony emerged, her body wrapped in a fluffy white bathrobe and her hair caught up in an equally fluffy towel.

"You're still here."

"You sound disappointed," Cass replied as he looked back at the book he'd plucked from one of her shelves. He'd barely read five pages of it.

"More just wondering why."

She sat in a chair near the fireplace and held out her hands to the flames. With her makeup washed off and her skin bare, she still looked beautiful, but more innocent, ethereal.

Guilt returned in full force. He'd dragged her into this life. If it hadn't been for his grand scheme, she wouldn't have been anywhere near that museum tonight.

"I'm still here because I needed to say I'm sorry."

Her head whipped around, her eyes widening in surprise.

"Sorry?" she repeated.

"If it hadn't been for me, you wouldn't have been at the museum tonight."

"Okay."

"And you wouldn't have been attacked."

She stared at him for a long moment.

"Do you feel…guilty?"

There was an odd note in her voice, but he ignored it, plowing forward with what he knew needed to be said.

"I do. Most of my thoughts were focused on the treaty and reclaiming my family's standing. Incidents like what happened tonight didn't even cross my mind."

"Cass, you couldn't have predicted this."

"I should have predicted this," he snapped back. "I should have anticipated something like this happening."

He'd spent the majority of the last nineteen years planning, ensuring that things would go right. When there was a plan, little could go wrong. When the details took center stage instead of emotions, there was little risk of failure. Even though so many people saw him as a playboy prince, in truth, he was a meticulous businessman who kept himself and those he allowed into his close circle in check.

But not tonight. Tonight he had been so focused on the stunning woman who had listened to a poor painter and finagled a brandy cocktail out of the bartender that he hadn't sensed the anger and resentment seething in the crowd outside until it had nearly been too late.

Yes, she was all right. But she could have not been. Those bruises could have been on her face if someone in the crowd had given in to their rage....

"Cass!"

He jerked out of the dark hole he'd descended into as one warm hand settled on his and another settled on his face.

"Are you okay?"

Briony's face came into focus, her eyes concerned, her brows drawn together in a worried frown.

"Yes." He started to push her away, but when he laid his hand on top of hers, his fingers slid across her skin. God help him, he couldn't pull away.

He wasn't sure who moved first. He didn't really care. All he knew was that one moment they were staring at each other and the next their lips were fused together in the most incredible kiss he'd ever experienced. He stood and pulled Briony to her feet, their mouths never parting as he gently unwound the towel from her hair and sank his hands into the damp tresses. She moaned, her lips parting beneath his as her hands slid under his jacket, her fingers splaying across his chest and burning through the material of his shirt.

His hand drifted down her neck, eliciting a sigh that filled him with an ecstasy he couldn't even begin to describe. His fingers drifted over the softness of her robe, grazed the base of her throat, then went lower still…until he paused. He wanted to feel her, all of her, finally claim what he had been dreaming about for weeks. But did he deserve it? She may have forgiven him for his deception, but she had one of the most innocent natures he'd ever encountered, despite the hardship life had dealt her. If he touched her, claimed her body after what he'd done, would that make him like the other monsters who had taken advantage of her?

Her back arched. One corner of her robe slid off her shoulder, and his fingers fell onto the full swell of her breast. He groaned as he cupped her in his hand, a finger sliding gently over her nipple and savoring the tightening as her hips thrust against his. Torn between wanting to relish the moment and wanting to see her naked, he wrenched his lips from hers. Her frustrated growl slid into a satisfied sigh as he pressed his mouth to her cheekbone, trailed his way down her neck and then captured one taut nipple in his mouth. Each suck, each delicate nibble, each moan made his blood burn so hot he was amazed they didn't both burst into flames.

As he turned his attention to her other breast, her own hands made quick work of the buttons on his shirt. He nearly came undone when her fingers found his bare chest.

"You feel so good," she murmured into his

hair as she struggled to tug his jacket, then his shirt off.

He lifted his head, ripped the clothes off his torso, then yanked the robe completely off her shoulders before he captured her in his arms once more. As her naked breasts pressed against his chest, he kissed her. Each press of his lips to hers spoke what he couldn't admit to himself...

You are mine.

When her hand drifted lower and slid down the growing bulge in his trousers, he groaned. Somehow, he summoned enough will to pull back.

"Briony...are you sure?"

She surged forward, throwing her arms around his neck as she kissed him again. He leaned down, slid his arms beneath her thighs and picked her up. He nearly lost it when she wrapped her long legs around his waist and pressed her body against his. They moved to the bed, tongues dueling, hands caressing, hearts pounding.

His legs hit the edge of the bed. He knelt down, slowly easing her back onto the mattress. Finally, she let go of her hold around his waist. He pulled back slightly, smoothed the hair back from her forehead. Emerald eyes glowed at him with a lust so intense he could barely stand the hardness between his thighs. He wanted to take her—*now*—but he would not rush. Not the first time he made his future wife truly his. He would erase every memory of any other man she'd ever been with. Regardless of the business nature of their arrangement, he would ensure that the intimate nature of their marriage would be more than satisfactory.

When he fully straightened, Briony let out a mewl of protest that quickly descended into a sigh of appreciation as he unzipped his pants and shoved them down his hips. Her eyes flared as he bared his body to his gaze.

At last, he was naked. Her appreciative smile made him feel like a god.

"You're beautiful." She winced. "I mean, handsome."

He chuckled as he knelt on the bed once more.

"Thank you. So are you." He slid one hand along the folds of her robe still tied about her waist. "Your turn."

Briony swallowed hard. Was she ready for this? Did she truly want tonight to be her first time? Just hours ago, she had been reminding herself to keep her distance from Cass, to not let herself get too involved.

As she looked up at Cass's magnificent body looming over hers, she knew with a certainty that yes, she wanted this. Needed this.

She smiled and nodded. Cass reached down, undid the belt of her robe and slowly parted the material. Her hands fisted in the silky sheets of the bed as she waited with bated breath.

"Stunning."

Her entire body warmed as Cass breathed out the one word. And then he moved with lightning speed to lean down, caging her between his arms as he sucked her nipple into his mouth. She arched off the bed with a little shriek as he made love to her breasts, sucking and nipping and kissing.

"Cass, please," she whispered as a tension started to build inside her, somewhere deep that made her ache.

He chuckled against her skin.

"Soon, *belle*."

His lips trailed lower, over her stomach and her hips, down farther still to the juncture of her thighs. When he kissed her *there*, she came undone, sensation spiraling through her body as she cried out and buried her hands in his hair, unable to take any more pleasure but not wanting him to stop.

Finally, her body went limp, sinking into the welcoming embrace of her bed as Cass trailed little kisses over her thighs, her hips, back up her stomach. He kissed each of her nipples, the slopes of her breasts, her neck.

"Briony."

She opened her eyes and smiled lazily at him. Was it even possible to feel so relaxed? So sated?

"That was incredible."

He smoothed her hair back from her forehead again, a simple gesture, but a tender one that made her eyes grow hot.

"Just wait."

Before she could reply, she felt his hardness press against her core. She sucked in a breath, anticipation and nervousness tangling together as she instinctively spread her thighs. When she felt him slowly start to slip in, she sighed with contentment as their bodies started to join. How amazing to feel him—

"Ow!"

She winced as he drove himself inside her. Cass froze, his eyes widening.

"Briony?"

"Mm-hmm?"

"Is there something you forgot to tell me?"

"Like what?"

"That you're a virgin?" Cass ground out.

"Was a virgin," she corrected.

"And you didn't think that was a pertinent fact?"

"I got a little distracted."

"You should have told me."

She sighed. "I wanted to give this to you."

He blinked, a subtle gesture but one that spoke volumes to her about how much her answer had surprised him.

"You what?"

She inhaled and then wiggled a little. The pain had already started to recede, leaving her with a full sensation between her legs.

Cass groaned. "Don't move."

"Isn't that what you're supposed to do?"

She couldn't tell whether he laughed or groaned.

"It is, but had I known you had never experienced this before, I would have handled things in a different manner."

She wriggled her hips once more. Not only had the pain nearly disappeared, but a little of the earlier excitement and sensation was slowly starting to return. Feeling emboldened by her new foray into the world of physical passion, she ran her fingers up over the backs of his thighs, over his rear and up his back. Cass sucked in a breath.

"Briony, if you keep that up, I might do something drastic."

She leaned up, thrilling to the sensation of the hair on his chest scraping against the delicate skin of her breasts.

"I'd love to feel something drastic," she whispered against his lips before she kissed him.

Cass didn't waste another minute. He withdrew from her, then slid back in with one long, agonizingly slow stroke. She raised her hips, trying to take him deep, deeper, deeper still as his tempo increased.

The tension returned, coiling even tighter as Cass moved inside her. Her hands drifted all over his body before coming up to frame his face.

"I love how you feel inside me."

Cass leaned down and kissed her, a raw, possessive passion that set off a chain reaction inside her. Heat burst between her thighs before spinning out through her veins, setting her nerve endings on fire as she cried out against his mouth. A few moments later, Cass groaned her name as he found his own release. He leaned down, pressed another gentle kiss to her lips and then rolled to the side.

She lay there for a moment, wondering what one did next in a situation like this. It was her room, so she wouldn't leave. Did she ask him to leave? Or would he just know to since he'd done this sort of thing before? Even if the thought of him leaving made her feel disappointed.

Cass slid an arm beneath her bare torso and pulled her across the bed. She gasped as his naked body pressed fully against her. He tucked her head into the crook of his arm, his hand drifting lazily through her hair.

"Tell me again why you decided not to mention that you had never been with another man."

"You distracted me."

She bit down on her lower lip. She was not going to make excuses or apologize for her lack of experience.

"So it's my fault?" he asked, a teasing note in his voice that relaxed her.

"Yes." She sighed again, a soft sound of satisfaction. "I feel like the last couple years of my life, people have wanted something from me. My relationships have been more transactional, what I could do for them."

Cass stiffened at her side.

"I wasn't any better."

"You were different. You told me up-front. Mostly up-front," she amended. "But you never portrayed our marriage as anything but what it would be." She rolled over and cupped his face. He flinched, but she didn't let him pull back.

"I know we'll never be a grand love story. I've accepted that. Tonight, before we went outside, I was enjoying my time with you. I've learned so much about myself, about what I want to do with my life and how I can make a difference here. I have you to thank for that." She smiled at him. "So much of my identity was caught up in my family, in being the person I thought they wanted so I could have their love, that I never bothered to ask what I wanted. And what I wanted tonight was you."

She rolled back onto her back and stared up at the ceiling, for some inexplicable reason slightly embarrassed by what she had to say next.

"I wanted you tonight. I know you wanted me, too, but you haven't pursued it. You haven't made sex a part of our agreement. That made me want it, and you, more. It wasn't transactional.

It didn't have any bearing on our contract." She inhaled deeply. "It was just...fun."

And soul-stirringly amazing. When the pain had faded and he'd started to move inside her, she felt not only the response of her body but the response of her heart. How long would she be able to keep her growing feelings for her future husband at bay?

"Fun," Cass repeated in a flat tone.

She turned her head and smiled at him.

"Very fun."

His chuckle sounded both surprised and a little nonplussed.

"I'm glad I could make your first experience fun."

They lay there for a moment in intimate silence. Her eyes drifted shut, and she was on her way to falling asleep when his voice broke the stillness.

"Why did you wait?"

"Hmm?"

"Why did you wait?"

"I was waiting for the man I would fall in love with," Briony murmured. "Since I can't have that, the next best thing is the man I'm marrying."

She registered the slight stiffening of his body.

But she was too tired to ask questions, too tired to do anything but let the pull of exhaustion take her into deep slumber.

CHAPTER THIRTEEN

CASS GLANCED AT Briony as she watched the numbers on the elevator light up, signaling their descent to the lower level of the palace. Tonight was the dinner with the ambassador from Switzerland and his family, as well as several other dignitaries. It was the final royal event not associated with the wedding. Clara had cleared their calendars next week for nothing but confirming details, completing rehearsals and keeping their time free for the "numerous last-minute things that are bound to come up," as Clara had put it.

He should be concerned that he was looking forward to spending more time with Briony. And not just time, but time confirming tablecloth colors and floral arrangements. His engagement was starting to feel all too real. He could better appreciate the emotional hell his aunt must have gone through because it was all too easy to submit to the temptation of a relationship.

It wasn't just that they'd had sex. Briony was

not one to linger in the background, reserving her time for shopping and lunch dates like his mother had. The same dedication she'd exhibited when taking care of her stepfamily had shown itself once more as she had taken her conversation with Hugo at the museum and run with it. Her committee had met every day in the past two weeks. She'd hosted a town hall for parents and even invited schoolchildren to the palace to share what they wanted out of their new school.

She was thriving. And the more she accomplished, the more captivated he became.

Even now, as she looked up at him with a small smile, Cass had to force himself to look away and not stare too much at his future bride.

Almost wife. In just over a month, she would be his wife. The past twenty-one days had flown by. The nights, however...

He'd woken up in Briony's bed after that first night to find it empty. He'd finally caught up with her in the ballroom with Clara discussing the timeline of their reception. Briony had been surprisingly distant. He didn't know what bothered him more, that he was bothered by her distance or that she had done exactly what she had said she would—not have any hope about theirs being any type of a love match.

A point made even worse by her words as she'd fallen asleep. He wasn't what she wanted, a man who could never fall in love. No, he was the "next best thing."

She deserved everything she wanted and more.

That night, he'd gone to bed alone. The following night, however, he'd been preparing for bed when a soft knock had sounded on his door. He'd opened it to find Briony in the hallway.

"I want you."

He should have said no. But he didn't, telling himself it was a natural part of their relationship, that they wouldn't produce heirs by practicing abstinence. Excuses, all, for what he knew deep down was the real reason: he wanted her just as badly. As soon as the door had closed, she'd thrown herself into his arms, kissing him with an unrestricted passion that had set his body on fire.

It had been much like that every night since. Meetings during the day, each of them pursuing their own royal agendas, and wild sex at night. Just last night, she'd sunk to her knees in the shower and taken him in her mouth, her tongue flicking over him as he'd fisted his hands in her hair and willed himself to hold on long enough to sink his length deep into her willing body.

He had everything he wanted laid before him: his revenge, the glimmers of hope for Linnaea's restoration, a fiancée who involved herself in the country's operations and who enjoyed sex almost as much as, if not more than, he did.

Yet with every shared laugh, every moment spent together, every casual caress, his uneasiness at his own lack of control and his guilt at how, once more, Briony had given up something she wanted grew.

The elevator doors slid open to reveal Clara, poised and ready as usual with her phone in one hand and tablet in another. But tonight, she looked different.

"You're wearing color," Cass said with surprise.

The tiniest blush tinged Clara's cheeks as she glanced down at the deep blue gown wrapped around her frame.

"Is it too much?"

He started to respond with his usual quips, but the uncertainty in her eyes stopped him.

"No. You look beautiful, Clara."

The pink deepened into red as her mouth curved up into the first real smile he'd ever seen on her. It transformed her entire visage and made him blink in surprise.

"Thank you, Your Highness." Clara directed her smile to Briony. "And thank you. I never would have worn it without your encouragement."

Briony reached out and squeezed Clara's hand as they started to walk down the hall.

"Cass is right. You look stunning."

Clara cleared her throat and pulled up a document on her tablet. Seconds later she was back to her usual self, rattling off facts about the upcoming dinner.

"You met his wife and daughter yesterday during lunch. His daughter is a student..."

Several minutes later, they reached the main dining room. Briony slid her hand into the crook of his elbow, a gesture that had become comforting and familiar. He reached down and squeezed her fingers.

"Ready?"

"Ready."

The dinner flew by. The Swiss ambassador and Alaric spent most of their time in quiet conversation at the head of the table. Briony chatted with the ambassador's wife and daughter. Cass spoke with two members of parliament at length about the trade agreements with Tulay. From what little he could hear of Daxon's conversations with the minister of the treasury, he was trying to make a case for money being allotted for a new resort in the mountains. Every now and then, he caught Briony's narrowed eyes as she glanced at her father.

How could the man be so blind? He had a son who would be a good leader for the people, a fact Cass had learned working so closely with Alaric the last three weeks. And he had a daughter who had not just overcome the most heart-wrenching disappointments but thrived as she continued to put others first.

The courses flew by: braised endive salad, scallops with caviar cream, and roasted venison with confit potatoes.

As their servers brought out plates of ginger cake topped with creamy icing and served with cinnamon apples on the side, Daxon's words carried across the table during a lull in the conversation.

"We could capture some of the tourists that go to Amsterdam or Rotterdam. We just need to make that initial investment."

"I think that's a great idea," Briony broke in.

Daxon smiled at her across the table, a smile that reminded Cass of a shark eyeing its prey.

"Thank you, my dear."

"Especially if the resort were to be located in Dhara or Candon," she continued. "I spoke with parents from those towns and their primary sources of income have all but dried up. A resort—"

"I would prefer to keep the resort close to Eira," Daxon interrupted, his smile turning patronizing. "It's a quaint notion, but Dhara and Candon have none of the luxury Eira can offer."

"I disagree. I haven't been to Dhara or Candon personally, and I would want to ensure the people would welcome a resort, but both areas offer mountains, lakes and towns that could thrive with an influx of tourist dollars."

Daxon's expression tightened, his skin stretching even further over his skull as he attempted to keep a smile on his face.

"Daughter, you've made quite an impression on the public, and some headway on your little project with the schools. That's good. But you don't have the experience to evaluate such a big investment."

"And I disagree with that."

Heads swung around to watch Cass as he speared Daxon with an icy gaze. His fingers tightened around the stem of his wineglass, the fragile material a reminder to keep a hold on his temper.

"Your daughter has proven to have an exceptional knack for evaluating Linnaea's weaknesses and proposing reasonable solutions that don't tax the treasury."

The barb hit its mark, Daxon's eyes narrowing to slits.

"While Eira has a lot to offer tourists, diversifying would be in our best interests to fully develop the entire country. And as Her Highness has said, getting the opinion of the people is paramount to success. It's why her work on the education system has been so widely welcomed. She has not only intelligence but a genuine interest in helping others."

"Not to mention time training in education with an American university," Alaric broke in.

"All excellent points." Everyone swung their gazes down to the Swiss ambassador, who nodded approvingly at Briony. "The Federal Council has admired the initial work being done to restore Linnaea's schools. It's still early, but if progress like that continues, I foresee a prosperous future for our two nations."

Daxon was many things, but he wasn't stupid. He inclined his head to Briony.

"My apologies, my dear. I certainly didn't mean to imply that you had not accomplished a great deal during your time here. And I welcome any suggestions you have on how to better benefit our rural regions."

Conversations slowly returned to normal around the table. Cass kept his eyes trained on Daxon, waiting in case the bastard chose to say something else foolish or hurtful. But the king simply resumed finishing his dessert.

Cass started as a hand wrapped around his under the table and squeezed. He glanced over to see Briony smiling at him with such warmth and affection in her emerald depths it made his chest ache.

"Thank you," she whispered.

You're in too deep.

He knew he was. He knew he had foolishly gone down the same path his aunt had, was succumbing too quickly to the emotions Briony created in him.

But when she made him feel like a knight in shining armor who could conquer the stars with just two simple words, how was he supposed to resist?

* * *

"You can call me Father at events like this, you know," Daxon said quietly with a smile that he probably meant to be paternal but instead looked forced. They had all gathered in the library after dinner and were enjoying cocktails as the evening wound down.

"I don't think we've spent enough time together for me to call you that just yet," Briony replied as kindly as she could manage.

Rage flashed in Daxon's eyes, an unexpected fire that transformed him from cool, distant monarch to almost unhinged. Her previous hurt over how they'd met and his cool distance in the prior weeks seemed like a faint memory. Why had she ever wanted a relationship with him?

"Don't cause a scene," he hissed.

"I'm not," she shot back. "You're the one who's about to embarrass yourself."

"At least I'm not marrying the nephew of a traitor," he spat back in a fierce whisper.

Her lips parted in shock. "From what Cass said, you spent money that wasn't yours. I would say that makes you the traitor."

"I was going to pay it back. I just needed more time." His lips tightened. "Alecine got everything she deserved and more, and so did that bastard of a brother of hers and his little brat. Cass's father fed her information, I'm sure of it. Had they stayed, I would have had them all thrown in prison for treason."

The depths of Daxon's viciousness, not to mention his complete lack of remorse, rendered her mute.

"Come now, my dear." Daxon's tight grip was no doubt leaving fingerprints on her waist. "She had to pay."

"Somehow I don't trust your version of events." She managed to push back and put some distance between them. "And even if she had, that was no reason to punish an eleven-year-old boy."

"If I had only gone after her, that wouldn't have sent a message. I needed to make it clear that no one would get away with crossing me."

Pride swelled in Bri's chest as her eyes found Cass. He stood on the edge of the room, arms crossed, eyes narrowed as he watched them talk.

"No one had the guts to stand up to you until Cass."

The rage returned, more intense than before. "He didn't stand up to me. He backed me into a corner. I had no choice but to agree."

"Agreed to use your own daughter as a bargaining chip to solve the problems you created."

"You're just like your mother," he sneered. "Idealistic. A dreamer."

"That's the best compliment anyone has ever given me."

She turned, about to walk away, then paused.

"I know now why Mom never told me about you. And I have to say, I'm glad."

With that parting comment, she walked away and circled the room, bidding good-night to the ambassador, his family and the other guests. Clara had fetched Alaric earlier. Judging by the glower on his face, it had not been for anything good. But before he'd quit the room, he'd come to her side and squeezed her hand.

"You are an integral part of this family now. Do not let our sire convince you otherwise."

Tears pricked her eyes. How could she have been so blind all these years, always fantasizing about the father she never had, pinning her hopes on Trey or reminiscing about the few good times she'd had with her stepsisters? All people who only gave out love if they got something they wanted. Transactional relationships she had gone along with, always focusing on what she didn't have instead of what she did, like the love of her mother who had gone to incredible lengths to keep her child safe.

Her gaze swung to Cass. He was talking with the minister of the treasury by the door, nodding at something the minister said but watching her with an intensity that made her catch her breath. Their relationship may have started out as a political alliance, but it had changed, deepened even before they'd made love. Tonight, when he'd defended her with pride in his voice, she'd known in that moment she was well and truly lost.

She was in love. She was in love with her future husband, and she didn't know what to do about it.

CHAPTER FOURTEEN

CASS BADE GOODNIGHT to the minister and the ambassador before he followed Briony out into the hall. As she'd been saying her goodbyes, he'd seen her eyes swing to him, a shell-shocked expression in her gaze. Before he could discern what was going on, she'd left.

"Briony."

Briony paused but didn't turn to face him. His eyes dipped down to her back, her skin visible beneath the turquoise lace. His exhale came out harsh. Now was not the time to be entertaining risqué thoughts.

"Are you all right?" he asked as he circled around and looked down at her.

She slowly raised her gaze up to his. Something flickered deep in her eyes.

"I am. It was just a longer night than I had anticipated."

"He had no right to embarrass you like that."

The corners of her mouth tilted up into a faint smile. "Thank you again for defending me."

"Of course."

Her face softened, her eyes coming alive with gratitude and that affection he'd glimpsed when she'd leaned over to whisper her thanks. It was a sight that both electrified and terrified him.

"It was the right thing to do."

Her head snapped back as if she'd been slapped.

"The right thing to do?" she repeated.

"Yes." His body tensed, muscles tightening as his heart tried to resist his rational mind taking over. "We need to present a united front and ensure there is no question of the work either of us is doing."

She stared at him, her gaze opaque. He stared back. She needed to stop putting him up on a damned white horse and turning him into her knight in shining armor. He wasn't a hero. He was a strategist, a survivor.

She circled around him and continued toward the elevator. He stood for a minute, frozen in place that she would reject him in such a manner. Yes, his response had been cold. But it didn't warrant such a cutting rejection.

He turned and started after her. As she got

into the elevator and saw him striding toward her, she regarded him with a burning gaze before reaching out and punching a button. The doors swished shut in his face.

He stared at the closed doors for a long moment. No one had ever walked away from him, much less closed a door in his face. He used the time the elevator traveled up and back down to breathe deeply and regain his sense of control. By the time he reached the doors to Briony's suite, he had his temper mostly back under control.

Mostly.

He knocked once.

"Go away."

He sighed as Briony's muffled voice traveled through the door.

"Briony, can we please talk?"

"There's nothing to talk about."

He tried the handle, surprised when it turned under his touch. The door swung open to reveal Briony slipping out of her dress, the material pooling about her feet and leaving her clad in nothing but black lace.

God, but she was beautiful. Slim legs, rounded hips, pert breasts straining against the cups of her bra. All he had to do was think about her and he stirred.

"Cass!"

She grabbed a blanket off the bed and wrapped it around her body.

"I did knock."

"And the door was closed!" she snapped.

"Should I go?"

She glared at him but didn't respond. He shut the door and walked into the room, taking slow, purposeful steps toward her. Judging by the blush creeping up her neck, she was just as affected as he was.

"In the Midwest, most people know a closed door means we don't want anyone coming in." Her teeth sank into her bottom lip as her gaze traveled down his body. Every step made him harder, amped up his desire until it took every ounce of willpower not to lunge forward and sweep her into his arms.

A distant warning sounded in his mind. This was what Aunt Alecine had told him about, this all-consuming passion that wiped out all rational thought and made one a fool. This was how she had fallen so low.

He pushed the warning away. He would address it later. Right now, he wanted her, his future wife, in his arms.

"You're not in the Midwest anymore, Briony." He stopped just a few inches away, not touching her, but inhaling her scent, savoring the heat from her body. Her quick inhale filled him with a want so deep he didn't know how he'd ever be able to sate it. "You're in Linnaea. And you're going to be my wife."

"A wife who will still slam the door in your face when you lie to me."

Her words were feisty, but her voice was breathy and heavy.

"I spoke the truth."

She shook her head. "I don't believe you. Why do you insist on keeping this distance between us? On trying to be the bad guy?"

He leaned down, his lips a heartbeat away from hers.

"I'm not trying, Briony. I am the bad guy."

With that, he kissed her. As soon as she started to kiss him back, he grabbed the blanket and wrenched it out of her grasp. She gasped as his hands trailed down her body, unclipping her bra in one quick movement and baring her breasts to his touch. She removed his tie with frantic grasps, then grabbed his shirt and ripped it down the middle, buttons flying across the room as she pressed her naked skin against his. He scooped her up into his arms and carried her to the thick rug in front of the fireplace. With the firelight dancing across her skin, her eyes glazed with passion as she reached up and cupped his face with her hand.

A thickness formed in his throat. When she looked at him like that, he wanted to be more than he was. He wanted to be capable of giving her what she wanted, the love story she deserved.

But since he couldn't do that, he could at least give her pleasure.

He removed the torn shirt, suit jacket and pants, then lay down next to her, sliding one arm beneath her body and cradling her against him. His fingers slid from her breasts, down her stomach to beneath the edge of the black lace panties that were driving him wild. He slid one finger down the middle of her molten heat, watching her face as her lips parted in ecstasy.

"Please!" she gasped.

He teased her, slipping one finger in and out, watching her arch and moan his name, her skin flushed as she neared the peak. Then, just before she went over the edge, he withdrew.

"Cass!" she half moaned, half laughed. He removed her panties, pressed a kiss to the sacred spot between her thighs, then moved up her body and slid inside her wet core, nearly coming undone as her body closed around him. He moved with slow, deliberate strokes, their tempo building as his body coiled, tight, tighter still. He would never get enough of her, could never have enough of the pleasure and joy she brought him.

She called out his name as she sailed into oblivion, wrapping her arms around him and hanging on as if he was her salvation instead of her curse. He whispered hers as he drove into her one last time as his release shuddered through his body.

He didn't know long they lay there, tangled in each other's bodies. When he finally raised his head, it was to see Briony looking up at him with questions in her eyes.

"What is it?"

"I've been doing a lot of thinking about my family. About Trey and the twins. My mom. Daxon."

He stroked a hand down her back, a touch designed to soothe away tension and provide comfort.

"A painful subject, I'm sure."

"I…" She sucked in a deep breath. "I have been focused on family for a long time, ever since my mom and Trey got married. At first it was trying to fit in and be who I thought Trey and the twins wanted me to be. How my mother loved me was the way all children should be loved, unconditionally."

"She should have seen that Trey wasn't being a good stepfather."

"Yes," Briony agreed with a nod. "But when she did confront him, I lied and pretended like everything was fine. I didn't want her to see how deeply Trey and I not forming a relationship hurt. After she passed, it went from trying to be who they wanted to trying to rescue them."

Cass smoothed a lock of hair out of her face, his hand lingering on her cheek. Her eyes fluttered shut as she pressed her face into his touch.

"Briony." He waited until she opened her eyes and met his gaze. He leaned down and touched his forehead to hers, the gesture somehow more intimate than many of the kisses he'd experienced in his life. "Your stepfather is a fool."

"He is," she agreed softly. "But so was I. I based myself on my family. I didn't take the time to get to know myself." She bowed her head. "And I thought that if I at least learned who my father was that it would make me whole. I was always looking for someone else to complete me."

Guilt hit him hard in the chest. His hand dropped from her face as he sat up and leaned back against the headboard, putting distance between them. He'd used her need to find out more about her family to manipulate her.

Coldness swept through him despite the warmth of the fire just feet away.

"I'm sorry things didn't turn out the way you wanted," he finally said.

Her hand came to rest on top of his. He watched with an almost horrified fascination as she wound her fingers through his, the emerald-and-topaz ring glinting in the firelight.

"I'm not."

His head jerked up. The tremulous smile on her face and the emotion brimming in her eyes set off dread in his heart that spread through his body like poison.

No. She can't possibly...

"Because your stepfamily is taken care of?" he asked with a casual indifference he didn't feel.

"No. Daxon turning out to be such a horrible person...it was freeing." She chuckled. "Learning what a horrible person he was, witnessing it for myself, it was like any desire I had to form a relationship with him just dried up. It was almost like when I made the decision to leave Kansas, as if chains had fallen off and I was suddenly free of this weight I'd created for myself. I had nothing but what I wanted out of my life. And the last couple of weeks, learning my royal duties, finding my passion again in working with the schools... I feel more like myself than I have since I was a child."

He suppressed a sigh of relief. Perhaps he had misunderstood what he'd read in her gaze. Perhaps she was just overcome with happiness at having a purpose.

"I'm glad."

"As am I." She brought his hand up, her fingers lightly dancing across his knuckles, the back of his hand in absent caresses that stoked the heat in his blood.

"Cass..." She sucked in a deep breath. "In finding my confidence, I also came to realize how important you've become to me. Not just because of what you've done for my stepfamily or because of what you're doing for Linnaea."

No. No, no, no.

"Briony—"

She placed a finger over his lips.

"Cass, please let me say this."

He watched her, not trusting himself to move. He would either kiss her senseless or flee. Neither option was a good one.

"I want to marry you, Cass. Not because I have to, but because I want to. I feel like I belong here, like I've found my home. Part of it is Linnaea, but a large part of it is you." Her smile grew wider. "Because I—"

"Stop!"

Cass stood in one swift motion and pushed Briony's hand away as he stalked over to the window. He stared out over the frozen landscape, his chest rising and falling as his heart raced. She'd been on the verge of saying it, saying the words that would ruin everything.

He focused on the line of trees in the distance, followed their trunks and snow-covered branches with his eyes as he slowly distanced himself from the emotions waging war inside his chest. When he'd at last regained control, he slowly turned to face Briony.

She sat on her bed amid a tangle of sheets, shoulders thrown back with the confidence of royalty. Pride surged through his defenses. She was more of a royal than Daxon could ever hope to be.

She would have made an excellent partner.

He acknowledged that thought with a measure of regret before he quashed it and buried it deep.

"I regret to inform you, Briony, that I must terminate our arrangement."

To her credit, she didn't dissolve into tears or throw a fit like other past lovers had. No, she just continued to stare at him, eyes searching for answers he couldn't give.

"Why?" she finally asked, her voice low and surprisingly emotionless given that just moments ago she'd been on the verge of saying something quite emotional.

"The dynamics of our relationship have changed. We will no longer suit."

"Because of what I almost just said?"

"Yes. I cannot return the sentiments you almost shared."

She cocked her head. "I believe you already have."

His chuckle filled the room, dark and caustic. "You're imagining things, Briony."

Her eyes narrowed. "Am I?" She tossed back the sheets and stood, crossing the room in measured steps. He tried to keep his gaze on her face and off the swells of her breasts, the nip of her waist, the curve of her thighs. Tried not to remember how perfectly she'd fit into his arms, how she'd made love to him with a trust and wild abandon he'd never experienced with any other lover.

"Your actions have spoken quite clearly in recent days."

"How so?"

"Spending time with me. Defending me in front of my father. Standing up for me to the paparazzi. Making love to me."

"Protecting my investment," he replied cruelly.

She stopped a mere foot away. Her sweet scent slid over his skin, sending a cascade of images through his head. Briony in her magnificent gown talking with a man just trying to survive. Briony refusing to back down in the face of the photographer. Briony standing up for the people of a country she hadn't even known existed a month ago. Briony, naked and shimmering beneath him as she cried out his name.

The ache of guilt was crushed beneath the weight of what he was about to do. What he had to do, he reminded himself as he summoned all of his strength. He couldn't give Briony what she wanted, what she deserved. She might consider herself in love with him now. But it wouldn't last when he couldn't return her affections. Their union would slowly dissolve from a respectful partnership to a prison of heartbreak and sorrow.

Briony had experienced enough of both to last a lifetime.

"How you held me just now," she whispered as she brought one hand up to touch his face.

He caught her wrist in an iron grasp.

"Briony, I used you. I've known for years how wretched Daxon is. I knew if I told you the truth, you'd never agree to the marriage contract."

"Why are you pushing me away?" she whispered.

"Because you love me and I don't love you."

The words had barely escaped before he longed to reach out and yank them back. Something felt wrong as he uttered them, a sense of imbalance deep in his soul.

Because you're a selfish bastard and you don't want to lose her.

Compassion and mercy blazed in her eyes, so strong and beautiful it almost hurt to look at her.

"Why can't you love me?" she asked softly.

"I've told you." He sounded ragged, torn up. The severity of his tone should have pushed her away, but damn it, she didn't back down.

"Yes, you have. Because of your aunt and your father. But you're not either of them, Cass."

She tugged her wrist free, and weakling that he was, he let her hand rest on his face, couldn't prevent the harsh exhale that escaped. Her palm warmed his skin, a simple touch but far more intimate than any liaison he'd ever experienced.

"I think your aunt and your father are just excuses."

His head snapped back, and he stepped out of her reach.

"Excuses?"

She threw back her shoulders, the confident woman he'd first fallen for in the bar standing in full force before him.

"I can't imagine experiencing what you did. But I think you're scared to be vulnerable. I think you use your aunt and father as a shield so you don't have to risk being hurt."

"Or I don't want to love you."

Silence fell. Even the crackling of the fireplace faded, overrun by the roaring in his ears that drowned out everything.

The words weren't entirely false. But they didn't tell the whole story. He didn't want to love Briony. But if he let himself, he would love her as he had never loved anyone, with his whole body and soul.

Briony was right. It wasn't just his father's

and aunt's doomed relationships that held him back. It was a volatile mix of his own cowardice, guilt and a fear that he wasn't the man Briony deserved.

Briony's face shuttered, her eyes going blank. He was doing the right thing. Trapping her in a loveless marriage would be liking trapping a wild bird in a cage and watching it beats its wings against the bars day after day.

"I've enjoyed our time together, Briony. But as of tonight, our engagement is over."

"What about Linnaea?" she finally asked.

Amazingly, she still sounded calm, in control. And, of course, was thinking about others instead of herself.

"I'll figure out something."

Even if he didn't have all the answers right now, he would find them. Briony might suffer in the short term, but one day she would look back and realize that he had set her free. When she had a husband who loved her and children of her own, she would be grateful.

Just the thought of another man touching her, let alone having children with her, made his blood boil with rage.

"I will, of course, provide you with funds, too, so that you may…"

His voice trailed off as she shook her head.

"No, thank you. I will swallow my pride to accept your generosity regarding Trey's treatment, the mortgage and the twins' funds. But anything else would make me feel…bought and paid for."

"You are not a whore," he ground out.

"No, I'm not. But I appreciate your concurrence. And how much you've helped my family. Thank you, Cass."

The words were gracious, her tone soft as she turned and walked away from him. He wanted to go after her, to reach out and touch her one last time, to tell her how much she'd helped him focus on the future and let go of the past.

But he couldn't. One touch and he'd be lost.

She started to pull on her dress.

"I'll go."

"No." She held up a hand. "I need to take a walk, clear my head."

She finished dressing and went to the door. Her hand reached out, grasped the handle.

Go. Go now.

She glanced back at him, and he nearly staggered at the depth of love shining in her eyes.

"I loved you because I wanted to, Cass. Not because I had to."

And then she was gone.

CHAPTER FIFTEEN

SHE HAD ONLY known this sense of heartbreak once: the moment her mother's hand had gone limp in her grasp as she'd breathed her last. She knew the feeling all too well. The numbness at first, the mind and heart both denying the evidence that lay right in front of her eyes. Then, slowly, the pain as reality trickled in, then broke through as if a dam had burst and an ache filled her entire body.

When she'd made the decision to tell him, she'd accepted that there was a strong possibility he would say he didn't love her. But she had comforted herself with the fact that at least she had tried, that it was better to tell him how she felt and risk that rejection than to cower like she had for so many years and not share what was in her heart.

She had not anticipated him ending their engagement. Now she had not only lost Cass but lost her ability to help Linnaea as well.

The elevator dinged, the doors swishing open to reveal the hallway where the royals kept their private offices. Alaric's was on the left. Her own was just past that on the right. Daxon maintained the most luxurious office at the end, although she'd never seen him enter it.

She started down the hall. Perhaps if she focused on some work, reviewing the feedback from parents from her town hall or a building proposal for a new school in the southern region, she could keep the pain at bay.

Everything was quiet. Almost quiet, she amended as she neared the door to Alaric's office. A strip of light was visible at the bottom of the door. She could barely make out the quiet murmur of two voices. Daxon had left as she'd been saying her goodbyes. Was he in the office with Alaric? She had no desire to see him again tonight.

She picked up her skirts and started to walk faster, hoping the tapping of her heels wouldn't be audible through the thick door.

So much for hope, she thought miserably as the door swung open.

"Briony?"

She turned and flashed a brittle smile at her brother.

"Sorry. Didn't mean to disturb you. I'm just heading to my room…"

Her voice trailed off as she caught sight of Clara standing behind Alaric. She drooped in relief.

"Where's Cassius?"

She blinked. "Cass? Oh, he's…um…well, that is to say…"

Clara surprised her by brushing past Alaric and coming up to lay a comforting hand on her shoulder. Her eyes were surprisingly kind.

"Did something happen?"

Briony swallowed hard.

"We…that is to say, Cass ended our engagement just now."

"What?" Alaric snapped. "Where is he? I'll—"

"Hush, Alaric," Clara said in a firm voice. "Briony, come inside, dear. Tell us what happened."

Briony let Clara lead her into the office and sit her down in one of the stiff-backed chairs in front of Alaric's desk. Alaric circled around and sat opposite her, steepling his fingers as he stared at her with his arctic gaze. Despite his power stance, he looked decidedly unsure of himself. If she hadn't been so upset, she would have found the sight of her older brother at a loss for words humorous.

"Why did Cass end the engagement?" Clara asked as she pressed a glass of water into Briony's hands.

Briony breathed in deeply. "I fell in love."

By the time she made it through the whole story, the painful ache had eased a fraction. Clara had filled her glass once, only interrupting here and there to ask a clarifying question. Alaric had watched her with a detached gaze the whole time.

Briony forced herself to swallow the rest of the water.

"I'm sorry, Alaric."

"Sorry?" he repeated softly.

"Without Cass's money, the country—"

"Damn his money."

Unlike his father, Alaric didn't need to raise his voice to be heard. The deep tones resonated with a barely suppressed fury that made Briony shiver.

"But—"

"I detested this arrangement from the start." He paused for a moment, as if trying to formulate his words. "But when I saw how the two of you were together, it convinced me that perhaps you could also be happy."

Briony smiled weakly. "For a brief time, I was."

Clara squeezed her hand. "Take it from me, Your Highness. You do not need a man or family to be happy."

Alaric frowned in his assistant's direction before he directed his attention back to Briony.

"The ambassador was impressed by what we've started to rebuild in such a short amount of time. Switzerland is ready to offer financial aid in exchange for several things we can offer, such as building a port along our northern coast. We won't get as much done as quickly as we would have with Cassius's money," Alaric admitted, "but we can still accomplish a great deal and become independent. You have not ruined this country, Briony. Far from it."

Relief swamped her. "Thank you."

"You're welcome. Now, what will make you happy?"

She knew the answer in an instant.

"I'd like to stay in Linnaea."

Alaric nodded. The look of pride on his face touched her.

"I'm glad," he said, and he sounded as if he

genuinely meant it. "I tend to do well with Linnaea's finances, laws, rules. The country could benefit from having someone who sees shades of gray, not just the black and white that has been my life."

Clara arched a brow as she tucked a long strand of white-blond hair behind her ear. "What an astute self-observation, Your Highness."

Alaric bowed his head. "Thank you."

Briony set the empty water glass on an end table.

"Thank you, Alaric. I don't know if Daxon will let me stay once the engagement is officially ended—"

"Let me worry about him."

Judging by the ice in Alaric's gaze, Daxon had a lot to answer for. There was a slight pang in Briony's chest that she had struck out twice when it came to father figures in her life. But then she released it. She may not have a father, or the man she'd fallen in love with, but she had a half brother she was coming to care for very much and, if Clara's unexpected support was anything to go by, another friend right here in the palace.

Really, she thought as a tiny seed of hope lodged in her chest, when she thought about it, she had a lot to be grateful for. The best part was she'd chosen all of it, not because she had to, not out of some misguided loyalty to family, but because she'd wanted it.

Briony stood.

"Thank you both. If you hadn't welcomed me in, I'd still be crying alone in my room."

Alaric stood and came around the desk. He grasped both her hands.

"He's a fool, Briony."

She nodded. "He is. But he's a fool who's hurting very deeply."

"No excuse," Alaric retorted.

But you don't know him like I do.

How could Cass even begin to compare himself to Daxon? Misguided, yes, and at times selfish. Yet in the time she'd come to know him, truly know him, she'd found that Prince Cassius Morgan Adama shared far more in common with Cass Morgan than probably even he himself realized. The man she'd started to fall for in Kansas had turned out to be so much more than she could have ever hoped for.

One day, she would be able to look back on that and smile knowing she had loved an incredible man.

"We'll agree to disagree," she said with a soft smile.

"For now. What else can I do?"

The idea popped into her head. At first it surprised her. But the more she thought about it, the more it felt right.

"Can you cover me for a couple days? There's someone I have to visit."

CHAPTER SIXTEEN

RAYS OF EARLY-MORNING sun filtered through the snow-covered trees. A whisper of a breeze trailed through the branches, releasing an occasional dusting that sparkled like fairy dust before it fell to the white ground. Somewhere deep in the woods, a bird tweeted a soft greeting. It was the kind of scenery painters rushed to capture and poets wrote odes to.

Cass barely noticed it as he wandered aimlessly through the snow. He didn't care about the beauty of his surroundings. If he focused on it too long, he would start to think about Briony, about how much she would love it and how she would probably lob a snowball at him when he wasn't looking.

You did the right thing.

He'd been playing that mantra in his head over and over again since last night. At first, it had done its job. It had stopped him from doing something rash like going after her. After the fourth shot of brandy had made the world tilt a little too much, he'd managed to sneak back to his room and fall into bed, his repetition providing some comfort as he drifted into a restless sleep.

But halfway through the night, when he'd awoken and reached out to touch her, only to have his hand graze the cold sheets, he'd had a moment of panic. How could he have let her go? Even if he couldn't return her love, he could have given her the world.

She doesn't want the world. She wants you. You don't deserve her after what you've done.

That reminder had made him put his phone down and lie back down. Even if he could overcome his decades-long commitment to never let himself make the same mistakes his aunt and father had, how could he begin to forgive himself for what he'd done to Briony? How had he ever thought that forcing her into marriage was better than what Daxon had done? Those thoughts had kept him tossing and turning until the first crack of dawn had finally roused him from his bed. Needing a distraction, he had donned his winter gear and traipsed out into the cold of a November morning before the majority of the palace had awakened. He'd avoided looking back, knowing his gaze would be drawn to a certain balcony and the room beyond.

Briony had fallen for a lie. She may not have realized it yet, but one day she would. And then not only would he still not be worthy of the incredible gift she had offered him, but she would leave. Leave like Daxon left Aunt Alecine. Leave like his mother had left his father.

Which just confirmed that he was a coward. That he would give in to his fear instead of take the risk like Briony had. Another confirmation that he wasn't good enough for her.

He circled around the north end of the small lake and headed back toward the palace, the sun climbing higher in the sky until it finally crested over the mountains. A golden glow bathed the landscape. It also obscured the figure moving swiftly toward him until the man was nearly upon him.

"It's difficult to kick you out of the palace when you're nowhere to be found."

Alaric's voice rang out across the field. Cass turned, resigned to whatever punishment Alaric was prepared to deal him.

"My apologies. I was on my way back. I can be in my room within twenty minutes if you'd like to schedule my eviction around then."

Alaric's curse reached him before he was able to blink the sun out of his eyes enough to see the prince's towering figure trudging through the snow. Alaric's face was a thundercloud, his lips stretched into a tight line.

"I would prefer to punch you."

Cass spread his gloved hands out. "I'll give you the first one for free."

Alaric snorted. "That wouldn't be as satisfying. Besides, a punch can't begin to compare to how much my sister is suffering."

A different kind of pain, sharp and cold, pierced his heart. It wasn't the pain of being out in the snow for too long. No, this was heartache at knowing he had hurt the one person he cared about more than anyone.

His eyes flew open as he straightened. He did care for Briony. Deeply. So much that he was prepared to give up the one thing he'd been working toward for nearly twenty years.

"I ended our engagement because I can't give her what she deserves."

Alaric arched a thick brow. "And what is that?"

"Love."

Alaric groaned and scrubbed a gloved hand over his face. He stomped over to a tree and leaned against it.

"I've seen the way you look at her, Cassius. You care for her."

"Of course I care for her," Cass growled. "How could I not?"

"So what is the difference between caring for and loving her?"

"Love can only last for so long before reality takes over. It may work for some people, but genuine affection and friendship last far longer in most cases."

"So why not give her that instead of making both of you miserable?"

"Because your sister thinks she loves me," Cass replied softly. "And she deserves to have someone who can give her something more in return than I'm capable of."

Alaric stared at him for a long moment. Cass returned his stare. He knew he was being evaluated, measured, on the verge of most likely being banished from Linnaea forever.

Strangely, that knowledge didn't make him feel angry or even desperate to find some way to stay. Unlike Aunt Alecine, he would deserve whatever happened to him. His dream of coming home, restoring his family's honor and reclaiming what had once been theirs seemed like a pale, distant memory compared to his past few weeks with Briony. Even after she had learned of his subterfuge, she had loved him, faults and all.

"I think, unfortunately, you and I are a lot alike."

Cass laughed. "Ah, yes. The jet-setting Mediterranean prince with a slew of broken hearts in his wake and the ice-cold heir apparent to the winter country of Linnaea. We could have been separated at birth."

"You don't love because you're scared."

His laugh abated as he slanted a glare at the older man. "Sounds like you talked to your sister last night. I have been many things in my life, but I've never made a decision out of fear."

Liar.

Alaric pushed himself off the tree and stalked closer. "You did last night. Briony offered you a gift, herself and her love, and it scared you. I know about your mother. I know what my father did to your aunt." He jabbed a finger in Cass's direction. "I think you based your decisions on what are obviously horrible examples of relationships, which makes you a damned fool. You kept yourself withdrawn, didn't get too deep into emotions and focused on other things like your revenge against Daxon."

A simmering anger started in Cass's stomach. "Speaking from experience, are we?"

Alaric froze, his eyes narrowing. Then, "Perhaps."

Cass shook his head. "What about your own fiancée, the one we never hear about?"

Alaric's jaw tightened. "Ours was a business arrangement. Necessity. Affection didn't play a part."

"That was what I had envisioned for myself."

But then I got to know your sister and she turned my world upside down. She is kind and strong and passionate. She deserves everything she ever wanted.

Alaric swore again and turned away.

"I can't help you. Not if you're going to remain steadfast in your belief that you can't love her in return." He stopped and looked over his shoulder. "And if you truly can't, then she's better off without you."

Cass balled his hands into fists. Why could Alaric of all people not see that he had done the right thing in setting Briony free to find true happiness?

"I expect you to be out of the palace by noon today," Alaric called over his shoulder. "Briony encouraged me not to void your reinstated citizenship, even though I could have since you terminated the contract when you ended the engagement."

"What if we signed a new contract?"

Alaric paused, then slowly turned back to face Cass.

"I don't want or need your money."

"Linnaea does."

"Not anymore. The Swiss ambassador has offered us financial aid."

"An offer that I'm sure is nowhere near as generous as the one I offered."

"We'll make do," Alaric ground out.

"Or you could listen to my new proposal, one that won't tie anyone down to any agreements and keep Linnaea on this new path."

As he said the words, Cass was filled with a sense of rightness that had been missing when he'd signed the contracts with Daxon and Alaric last month, and when he'd signed the contract with Briony. On those days, his thirst for revenge had overridden what the focus should have been on.

But now, in this moment, he knew he was doing the right thing. Not to exact revenge, not to secure a place for his family, but because it was the right thing to do for his country.

"What are you proposing?"

Alaric's voice was cautious, his face a solemn mask.

"Everything we've discussed the past few weeks, minus the marriage. I won't force Briony into another agreement against her will. My only condition is that my arrangement be with you and not Daxon."

A grim smile crossed Alaric's face. "After all this time, you would give up your revenge?"

Cass shrugged as he started walking. "It never should have been about revenge in the first place. Once the details are taken care of, I'll be leaving for Tulay."

Alaric fell into step beside him. "You're just going to leave?"

"Yes." After last night's disaster, Linnaea no longer felt like home. Neither did Tulay. Perhaps he would never find a place to call home.

Alaric shook his head again.

"You're a fool, Cassius. A damned fool."

CHAPTER SEVENTEEN

BRIONY WALKED AROUND the interior of the Ledge as she soaked up the memories of the past eighteen months. It hadn't been her dream job, but for a long time it had been an escape. It had become one of the few constants in her life, and for that, she would always be grateful. She had spent so much time lamenting the lack of affection from her stepfather and stepsisters that she hadn't fully appreciated the people who had made that time bearable.

Time didn't erase the vivid memory of the last time she'd seen Cass as he'd tried to push her. Despite his cruel words, she'd seen his own emotions in his eyes. He loved her, of that she was certain.

But she was done waiting for people to treat her the way she deserved to be treated. If Cass preferred to deny how he felt and chose living in his emotionless world, and if she truly loved him, then she had to respect his choice. To force him to do anything would make her a monster in her own way. And it would wipe away the strength she'd discovered in herself this past week. To live her life pining for someone else and placing her entire happiness in his hands would be falling right back into a pattern she'd only just begun to break free of.

Knowing she had made significant changes would one day bolster her spirits. But for now, it served as the most minimal of cold comforts.

Gus came out of the back, wiping his burly hands on a towel.

"Still can't believe we had an actual princess slinging drinks," he said with a gap-toothed grin that flashed white against his dark brown skin.

"I don't think I was technically a princess at the time," she replied with a small laugh.

"Kim says you better come say goodbye before you go back so she can curtsy to you. And so she can tell Lisa that she met a real princess when she was a baby."

"I'm in town through tomorrow, so I can definitely do that."

Gus's face sobered. "How's the stepfamily?"

A sense of peace filled Briony's chest. "Surprisingly decent. Trey's out of rehab and back home. He has a job interview next week with his old company."

Gus's eyebrows shot up. "Well, least it's something."

"It is. And he even apologized."

After she'd made the decision to fly back to Kansas, pack up her remaining things and say goodbye to her coworkers, she'd texted Trey and the twins to let them know. Trey had surprised her by calling her. He'd thanked her for getting him help and then surprised her even more with a heartfelt apology, not just for the months since Mom had died, but for how he'd failed her as a stepfather.

"I thought treating you nice was enough," he'd said, sorrow heavy in his voice. "After your mother died, I got angry. Angry that your mom wasn't there to see us, angry that you were so much like her. It's no excuse," he'd added quickly. "I just need you to know it wasn't you."

Even though she'd already known that, hearing it from Trey had been a balm to the wounds she'd sustained. They would never be close. But it was better than anything they'd ever had.

Gus grunted. "Bet he's playing nice so he can try to finagle some money out of you."

"I wondered so, too. But money hasn't come

up since we started talking again. Maybe I'm being naive, but I'd like to think he's becoming a better man."

It had been nice, too, hearing that Mom had actually told Trey about her history with Daxon. She'd even left a packet of letters for Briony to read, letters she hadn't quite been able to read yet. But soon.

"And the twins?"

Briony's smile grew. Ella had surprised her by throwing her arms around Briony when she'd stopped by to pick up the letters, sobbing and asking for forgiveness for her horrible behavior. Stacy had been a little more reserved, but had echoed her sister's apology and even given Briony a gift—a necklace of her mother's she'd found in the attic.

"Apparently Trey's sister Debra was just what they needed. I made too many excuses for them and let them get away with too much for far too long. Between the chores, grocery shopping and getting grounded for not doing their homework, they had a rough few weeks."

Not that Debra had done it out of any great love. As she'd told Briony as she'd thrown the last of her suitcases in the trunk, "I got sick of the whining."

Gus rolled his eyes. "How many times did I tell you that you were too easy on all of them?"

Briony held up her hands in surrender. "And you were right." She leaned up on her tiptoes and pressed a kiss to the owner's cheek. "You're a great dad, Gus."

Gus flushed with pleasure. "Thanks." He glanced at the clock. "Four o'clock. Sure I can't convince you to work one last shift?"

"No, thanks. But I'll stay for a bit."

As Gus opened the doors and a few customers poured in, Briony hung off to the side. Some of the regulars came up to her to congratulate her on her engagement. She managed to paste a smile on her face and thank them. A couple asked for selfies, which she grudgingly obliged.

Yes, things had definitely changed, she mused as the bar started to crowd up. People still waved and were friendly. But there were plenty more side glances, whispers behind hands and people trying to covertly snap her photo. Fortunately, she was leaving later that evening. It wouldn't be too long before the photos made the rounds online and an enterprising paparazzo or two came knocking.

For a moment, she thought back to that Thursday just before three o'clock when she'd been alone in the bar pulling chairs off tables. The last minute her life had been somewhat normal. Despite the yuckiness of her situation at home, she had been anonymous, just one person moving in a sea of billions worldwide.

And then Cass had walked in.

Her eyes drifted toward the door before she could stop herself. She'd been gone three days. The first day, she'd spent the plane ride back to the US grabbing her phone every time it dinged.

No text messages. No phone calls. No emails. Nothing.

The second day, she'd perused the newspapers, waiting for news of their broken engagement to circulate. Except it hadn't. Aside from photos of the ball, there had been no news of Linnaea or Cass.

She'd called Clara to ask what had happened. With the wedding just four weeks away, she thought the palace would have released a statement as far in advance as possible.

"We'll make the announcement at the appropriate time," had been Clara's cryptic reply. She'd then told Briony to stop worrying and enjoy her time in Kansas.

She'd tried. She'd tried very hard, but in moments like these, when she had little to distract her, it was very hard to prevent her thoughts from drifting to Cass and the last time he'd held her in his arms. To close her eyes and remember how gentle he'd been with the children when they'd toured the wing of the hospital that would be upgraded to a pediatric unit. As he'd crouched down to admire a little boy's cast and sign his name, she'd known what a wonderful father he'd make.

Stop.

Cass was out of her life. Perhaps one day she could stomach the thought of going on a date with someone else. Although whether that person would be interested in her or her new status, she would probably always wonder.

Not to mention the thought of sharing a romantic meal, let alone holding hands or, God forbid, kissing someone else made her sick to her stomach.

Maybe I could adopt. The thought gave her a much-needed boost of happiness. Between that and her work with Linnaea's schools, she could have a full life.

And the more time that passed, the more she'd be able to visit her memories of Cass and smile with nostalgic longing instead of swallowing back tears of heartache.

Gus turned the televisions on in preparation for the game. Briony glanced at one of the screens, then did a double take.

"Wait, Gus, go back!"

Gus clicked back to the first channel. A picture of her and Cass was featured in the corner. The news anchor's mouth was moving, but she could barely hear what was being said.

"Turn it up!"

Moments later, the anchor's deep voice reached her ears over the din of the bar.

"...Morgan Adama of Tulay released a joint statement with his soon-to-be brother-in-law, Prince Alaric Van Ambrose of Linnaea. Prince Cassius is engaged to Prince Alaric's long-lost half sister, Princess Briony Anne Van Ambrose."

The screen filled with an image of Cass and Alaric standing next to each other at a lectern in front of the grand entrance to the palace. Her throat tightened as her heart started to pound furiously. Despite the dark circles beneath his eyes, Cass still looked incredibly handsome in a navy suit and brown tie that brought out the amber in his gaze.

"Prince Cassius and I have renegotiated the terms of the financial agreement between Linnaea and Tulay. The previous draft was an alliance based on his marriage to my sister, Princess Briony. The provision of marriage has been struck from the contract."

Her stomach dropped. This was it. The entire bar, let alone the world, was going to learn that her engagement was over.

Someone from the audience in front of the palace shouted a question. Cass stepped up to the lectern. Briony turned away, tears blurring her vision as she started for the back. If she was going to cry, she was going to do so in private.

"Prince Alaric and I reached this agreement because I want my future wife to know that I am marrying her for her and her alone."

Briony froze. Then, slowly, she turned, her eyes riveted on the screen as a cautious hope filled her chest.

Another indiscernible question was asked. Cass looked straight at the camera.

"I am very much looking forward to an alliance between Tulay and Linnaea. But I would be lying if I said I wasn't looking forward to my wedding the most."

"I meant every word." She heard him speak, this time much clearer, much closer.

His voice washed over her, deep and smooth like a fine whiskey. She wanted to turn, but it was as if roots sprang from the ground and wrapped around her feet. She couldn't move, couldn't breathe.

Awareness swept over her with a crackling intensity as she felt him come closer, felt the heat of his body as he stopped mere inches away.

"I missed you, Briony."

Slowly, ever so slowly, she turned and looked up to meet Cass's smoldering golden-brown gaze.

"Did you?"

"Very much."

She swallowed hard. "I'm a surprised to see you here given the way our last conversation went."

"I imagine you are."

He breathed in and she realized Cass was nervous. The thought made a laugh rise in her throat that she barely bit back in time.

"It's rather crowded in here," Cass said as he cast an eye over the bar.

"Football game tonight."

He rolled his eyes. "I forgot how you Americans use the wrong name for your sports."

Briony arched an eyebrow as she folded her arms over her chest. "You came all this way to criticize one of our favorite pastimes?"

Before she could pull back, he cupped her cheek. The shock of his bare skin on hers after several days apart electrified her senses as she instinctively leaned into his touch. He bent down.

"No," he murmured, the warmth of his breath brushing her ear. "I came all this way for you."

CHAPTER EIGHTEEN

CASS WAITED WITH bated breath as Briony watched him with an opaque stare. She would be well within her rights to have him tossed out of the bar and tell him she never wanted to see him again. The thought made him press his hand more firmly against her cheek. If this was going to be the last time he got to touch her, he would soak up every moment he could.

"We can talk on the patio," she finally said.

Relief spiraled through him. Talking was a start.

Briony led him through the crowds. He spotted more than one curious stare, and a couple people snapping photos. He grimaced. One of the positives of living in security-tight Linnaea the past month had been not having to worry about the media or a wayward tourist snapping his photo. Who would have thought he'd have to worry about such things in the middle of a Midwestern prairie?

The patio was mercifully empty. Surrounded on three sides by a wooden privacy fence and dotted with chairs and tables, the patio was covered in snow. With a string of lights casting a glow on the snow and a lone firepit flickering in the center, it offered a cozy and intimate atmosphere. Perfect for what he had to say.

And if Briony walked out of his life after she'd listened to him, he'd have somewhere private to mourn.

Briony brushed some snow off one of the chairs and sat, holding her hands out to the fire. She kept her gaze focused on the flames. The light brought out the gold intertwined in her strands of red.

When it seemed like she had no intention of saying anything, he decided to plow forward.

"You saw the press conference."

"I did."

Her tone betrayed nothing. No anger, no sadness, no happiness. Her face remained a blank mask.

"What did you think?"

"It was surprising."

He stifled his initial irritation at her oblique answers. It was no more than he deserved.

"I did it for two reasons." He moved toward

the fire and sat down in the chair next to her. When she didn't move away from him, he took it as a positive sign. "You were right, Briony."

That got her attention. She turned to look at him, a quizzical look on her beautiful face.

"Tying my offer of help to marriage wasn't a means of protecting my finances or ensuring the money was properly spent. It was part of my revenge."

The bleakness that appeared in her eyes made him hurry on.

"That was how I saw it when I made the offer to Daxon. I reasoned that because I would be helping a country, and rescuing you from a poor financial situation, it was okay for me to get some benefit, too." His voice turned bitter as he forced out the words. "I saw myself as a knight in shining armor for both you and Linnaea. I was so proud of myself for intertwining my revenge with what I saw as helping that I didn't stop to think about how my motivations tainted what I was doing."

Briony reached over and laid a hand on his knee. Just that simple touch, her gloved hand on his leg, nearly made him reach over and haul her onto his lap. But there was too much left unsaid. And if she did decide to not kick him out of her life forever, it had to be her choice, not him forcing her.

"I started to realize what I was doing was unfair when I first got to know you. Because you weren't some helpless damsel in distress. You were a living, breathing, compassionate woman who worked hard to provide for her family, harder than I ever have."

"I find that hard to believe," Briony said softly with a small but kind smile. "You wouldn't have the wealth you do without some hard work."

"Wealth that got a very generous start from my Aunt Alecine's husband." Slowly, he laid his hand on top of hers and murmured a silent prayer of thanks when she didn't pull away. "The more I got to know you, and the more I worked with your brother, the more my focus started to shift. It was no longer about punishing your father. It started to be about what it should have been all along—helping the country avoid a depression and regain its footing."

Briony's lips parted, but then she looked away.

"What is it?"

"It just…if things started to change, why did you…"

"Send you away?"

She nodded, her gaze still focused off to the

side. He ached to hold her, to comfort her and wipe away all the pain he had caused her.

"Because I fell in love with you."

For a moment, he wondered if she'd heard him because she just continued to stare into the fire. But then slowly, so slowly it nearly tore him apart, she turned to look at him, her eyes wide, lips slightly parted.

"What?"

"I fell in love with you," he repeated. "And it was wonderful and terrifying. The guilt I'd been feeling since I met you took over. I felt like I was just as bad as, if not worse than, your father."

"How could you possibly be worse?"

"Because he has no conscience. I have at least somewhat of a conscience, and I still proceeded to pressure you into getting engaged and leaving your life behind."

Briony shook her head. "You offered me a choice."

"Between redemption and devastation." No longer able to stop himself from touching her, he slid his gloves off. Then, with slow movements, he slid hers off as well. Her breathing quickened as a blush crept over her cheeks. Slowly, ever so slowly, he entwined his fingers with hers, his heart racing as if he were a teenage boy on his first date. Amazing how Briony brought even the simplest of things to life.

"You're being too hard on yourself, Cass."

"I'm not, Briony. And it wasn't just how I'd treated you." He frowned, remembering Alaric's too-accurate analysis of his history. "I've never felt about anyone the way I've felt about you. The one example I've had of so-called love ended in devastation for my entire family. My aunt and father described such emotions as weakness. It's hard to rework one's lifelong views in such a short time, especially when guilt weighs you down."

"What changed?"

Cass smiled ruefully. "Your brother started me down the right path."

"My brother?" Briony repeated disbelievingly.

"After he threatened to punch me."

Her eyes swept over his face. "Did he actually hit you?"

His hand came up and cupped her cheek once more. "Not physically. But emotionally, yes. He told me how foolish I was, that it was evident how much I cared for you. I resisted at first. But I offered to rework the contract so the financial agreement would no longer be tied to our marriage."

"Why?" she whispered.

"Because it was the right thing to do. And," he added as he leaned in, "because as your brother and I were talking, all I could think about was you. Linnaea no longer felt like home. Tulay didn't, either. When I thought of home, I thought of you. Once I realized what that meant, I knew removing the marriage stipulation from the agreement not only was the right thing to do, but it would give you the true choice I never gave you in the first place."

"Oh, Cass."

"Linnaea and Tulay have officially entered into an agreement that will provide substantial funds for Linnaea's recovery. Your stepfather's treatment is paid for, including a year's worth of counseling services. Your stepsisters have full college funds, and the mortgage has been paid in full."

A single tear slid down her cheek. He released one of her hands and wiped it away.

"Please don't cry, Briony."

"You've been so generous," she said shakily as another tear fell.

"No, I haven't. It's what I should have done all along without holding an engagement ring to your head."

"Cass…"

He put a finger to her lips.

"One last thing, Briony, and then I promise to be silent for whatever you have to say." He came out of his chair, got down on one knee and reached into his pocket. Briony gasped as he pulled out a black velvet box and popped the lid. Nestled inside was her engagement ring, the emerald-and-topaz stones winking up at them.

"Briony, I love you. You've brought joy to my life. You've already made me a better man and a better leader. Would you do me the honor of becoming my wife and making me a husband?"

Tears were now cascading down her cheeks.

"Are you crying because you're happy or because I've ruined any chance I ever had?"

With a deep sob she flung herself forward and wrapped her arms around his neck. His arms flew around her and crushed her to his chest.

"Briony," he breathed into her hair, inhaling her intoxicating scent, "is that a yes?"

She pulled back and framed his face between her hands. "Yes! Yes, yes, yes!" She pressed her lips to his. Hunger and love surged through him as he buried one hand in her hair and poured all of his emotion into their embrace. His mouth moved over hers, claiming her with every touch.

At last, they emerged for a breath. Cass slipped the ring on her finger and pressed a kiss to her knuckles. But, as her gaze moved from her ring back up to his face, he realized that even though Briony had accepted his proposal, she still hadn't told him how she felt.

As if she could read his mind, she gave him the most incredible smile.

"I love you, Cass."

He swallowed hard past the thickness in his throat. "Truly?"

"Oh, yes. I had already started to fall in love with you when you were plain Cass Morgan. And when you stood up for me, and encouraged my ideas, and saw the real me, I fell in love with Prince Cassius."

He pressed a kiss to the tip of her nose, then her cheeks, then once more on her lips, savoring her sweet sigh of contentment.

"I know your brother flew you here on the royal plane. But I think it would make much more sense for you to fly home with me."

The smile that lit up her face made him feel like he could move mountains.

"Home," she echoed. "That sounds wonderful."

EPILOGUE

BRIONY STARED AT herself once more in the mirror. But today, instead of gazing at her reflection with trepidation, she felt as if she could fly, she was so happy.

The designer had fashioned a gold creation, vines intertwining over the strapless bodice before cascading down onto the full, fluffy skirt. Matching gold slippers peeped out from beneath the material. A stylist had made her curls gleam beneath the matching veil. The florist had put together burgundy and white flowers that stood out beautifully against the gown.

Her hand drifted down to her stomach, still flat beneath the dress.

But not for long, she thought with a small, secret smile. She'd taken the test that morning. Cass would be getting quite the wedding present that evening.

A brief knock sounded a moment before Clara walked in. Dressed in a midnight-blue shift dress, flats, her hair pulled back into her signature tight bun at the base of her neck and a clipboard in hand, she looked every inch the personal concierge of the prince.

Except, Briony noted with some concern, she looked awfully pale, with dark half-moons beneath her eyes.

"Are you all right, Clara?"

Clara gave her a wan smile. "Yes, just feeling a little under the weather."

One hand came off the clipboard and drifted down to land on her stomach. Briony froze, then looked away as the puzzle pieces clicked into place. The night of the dinner for the Swiss ambassador, Alaric's fiancée had ended their engagement, a fact Briony had learned about after she'd returned from Kansas.

Memories of that night flashed through her mind, details she had missed as she'd focused on her own grief. Clara's unbound hair, Alaric's slightly mussed shirt.

Apparently, Alaric and Cass were going to have even more in common.

"I appreciate all you're doing."

Clara nodded, then slipped back into planning mode.

"Ten minutes and Prince Alaric will be here

to walk you down to the chapel. We'll line up outside the doors at a quarter to five. The doors will open at five exactly."

When Alaric had offered to walk her down the aisle, Briony had barely stopped herself from bursting into tears. Who would have thought that just when she started focusing on other things in her life, she would be gifted a family?

Daxon hadn't taken too kindly to her turning down his offer to walk her down the aisle. But Clara, bless her, had arranged for Daxon to welcome guests to the ceremony, a role that had assuaged his ego enough that he hadn't made a fuss since. Trey, the twins and the employees of the Ledge had even been flown in as guests.

Briony stepped down from the dais and wrapped Clara in a hug. Clara froze, then slowly hugged her back.

"Thank you, Clara." She leaned back. "For everything."

Clara's face relaxed into a genuine smile. "Of course. Prince Cassius and Prince Alaric are both lucky to have you in their lives."

Clara hurried out, leaving Briony alone in her suite for a blessed few moments of peace and quiet. She went back up on the dais and spun in a circle. The skirt flared out before coming to rest against her legs. Her mom would have loved it. Another knock sounded on the door. Briony stepped down and crossed the room. Perhaps Clara had forgotten something.

"Who is it?"

"Your future husband."

His voice washed over her and ignited the heat that flared to life every time she heard his voice.

"It's bad luck to see the bride before the wedding."

"My eyes are closed."

She should send him away. But that would just be spiting herself. She slowly opened the door, making sure his eyes were truly shut, before she threw herself into his arms. He caught her and wrapped her in a strong hug that made her feel cherished.

"You feel beautiful."

"How can one feel beautiful?" she asked with a laugh.

"I don't know, but you do."

She leaned into him, inhaling his scent and soaking in his warmth.

"I have a surprise for you," she whispered, unable to contain her excitement anymore.

His hands slipped down and cupped her backside.

"Does it have something to do with what's under your dress?"

She laughed. "Yes, but not what you're thinking. Promise to keep your eyes closed?"

After he nodded, she grabbed one of his hands and guided it to her stomach. His fingers fell flat on her belly, a frown crossing his face before he froze.

"Briony…really?"

"Really."

With an exultant shout, he picked her up and spun her around in a circle as she shrieked with laughter.

"No peeking!"

"I'm not!"

He set her down and kissed her with a fervor that made her head spin.

"You're pregnant. And you're going to be my wife," he whispered reverently as his hand drifted back to her stomach, his fingers drifting across in a soft caress.

"I love you."

"And I love you, Briony. Always."

* * * * *

LET'S TALK

Romance

For exclusive extracts, competitions
and special offers, find us online:

- **f** facebook.com/millsandboon
- **◎** @millsandboonuk
- **🐦** @millsandboon

Or get in touch on 0844 844 1351*

For all the latest titles coming soon,
visit millsandboon.co.uk/nextmonth

*Calls cost 7p per minute plus your phone company's price per
minute access charge